TRUTH LIES & SEAGULLS

AN ANTHOLOGY

CONTENTS

Foreword vii

RIDERS ON THE STORM 1
Mike Lamborn

INSERT COIN 10
Alex Delve

THE PIER, MS AND ME 20
Kay-Anne Sheen

THE GARRISON 29
C. Ellis-Ballinger

NO PLACE LIKE HOME 38
Steven Rosen

GHOST ON THE PIER 48
Catherine Thornton

PETER PAN NEVER GREW UP 50
Belle Harper

GOOD WIND 60
Abigail Keys

THE TWITCH MARCH 71
Diann Webb

JUDGEMENT DAY 81
Richard Kurti

NEVER NEVER LAND 93
Catherine Thornton

GROWING UP IN LEIGH-ON-SEA 95
Jim Riches

SPANISH ESTATE 104
Carolin Voigt

SLEEPING BEAUTY STIRS 109
Adrian Lacey

THE MEETINGS 118
Rachel Dingle

In Support Of 129

Aspirations Program 131
The Essex Wildlife Trust 133
Acknowledgments 135

TRUTH, LIES & SEAGULLS

First Published by Write Club/ Create 98 and Cockney Prophet Publications 2023

Cover Layout and Design by Simon Fowler of Create 98

Typeset by Alex Delve in Palatino

ISBN: 978-1-7391551-9-3

FOREWORD

What a joy it is to introduce this, a collection of short stories written around Southend.

Write Club was the brain child of Richard, Jen and I in 2019. Our focus was on getting potential writers together to learn and practise writing with a real focus on publication. We tutored story-telling skills and aspects of the publishing industry and had brilliant guest speakers including writers, agents, editors. Several of our students have gone on to publish their work but this is Write Club's first anthology. And it's a cracker.

I didn't work on this collection - I bowed out last summer to concentrate on my own writing which left Richard to single-handedly steer this ship - kudos to him - he's done a fantastic job. I know how much work and love has gone into it.

Over the last few years, Southend has undergone some major transformations too - becoming a city following the murder of Sir David Amess MP, difficulties with the football club, pollution in the estuary, pier of the year, crime, tourism, new-developments or not, parking issues - there is a lot! We writers often talk about how 'place' is a character - by which we mean setting should be treated with as much attention to detail and as much influence as any main character in your story - well, what characters these authors have given us. The good, the bad and the ugly are all here! I love that this collection is a really stripped back, authentic look at our town, sorry, city.

In many ways, it reflects Southend's unique personality: We're not afraid to look at what lies underneath - just as we can see the mud when the tide is out - but there's hope here too - in the same way we can always see land the other side.

I'm not going to single out any favourites here, they're all brilliant. Oh alright, if I must, I particularly loved Rachel's eviscerating account of meetings - having attended a few like this myself, it was instantly recognisable - and I loved the humour in Adrian's Sleeping Beauty. I know you'll find some favourites in here too - let them know! If writers have a fatal flaw it is their love of feedback and reviews.

I'm writing this in another tumultuous week when inhumanity and brutality seems to be winning, yet, reading these stories, I find myself heartened. Here is the antidote - here is the humanity. These tales of community, empathy and memory. These writers with passion, imagination and ambition. It's all here - so feast your eyes, kiss me quick and dig in...

Samantha Lierens (aka Lizzie Page)

RIDERS ON THE STORM

MIKE LAMBORN

He checks the forecast before bed; still gales, a red warning.

He sleeps fitfully, hearing the wind rattling around the house.

He wakes early, a bit bleary eyed to dull morning light.

Draws the curtains to see swaying trees, clouds scudding across a grey leaden sky.

Not a spec of blue in sight.

Making tea, he stares out of the kitchen window, he ponders

How much wind is there?

Will it decline, will it increase?

Which board and sail will I need today?

WhatsApp messages pinging;

It's going to be a windy one.

See everyone down there.

Be safe, it's going to be wild.

Excitement, with a sliver of apprehension as he hears the wind howling.

Tempting him.

A siren's call.

Into the van, he feels the wind rock it slightly. Slurping tea from his Keepcup, still hot and steaming, crunching peanut butter toast between slurps, ignoring the crumbs cascading into his lap and onto the van floor, he double-checks he has everything.

Nothing forgotten.

He drives the short distance to the beach; sees leaves and other rubbish whipped up into the air, swirling, twirling, pirouetting; dancing madly in the road in front of him.

Streets are empty.

Only a few cars.

A tree has come down in someone's garden.

Seems to have missed the house.

Bushes and trees violently swaying, shaking and rustling.

Branches waving like wild flailing arms.

Roots cling to the ground despite the tug of the storm's sharp claws.

Parks at Chalkwell beach. He's not the first; a few early-birds already rigging up on the green.

He steps from the van and sees the waves

Rising.

Falling.

Tumbling.

The frothing white windblown spume like white icing splashed randomly on deep green marzipan waves, as the angry sea churns in front of him.

He looks up and sees the gulls.

Black flecked white dots against a grey sky ceiling.

Screeching.

Swooping.

Soaring.

Seemingly untroubled by the wall of wind.

The wind roars its warning; or is it daring?

A challenge laid down.

Wind blowing west to east.

Tide still rising.

Endless cloud rushing towards him.

He handles his kit over the wall onto the green's faded grass.

Others before him are ready to go, he takes a mental note of their sail sizes and pauses rigging-up to watch them set off.

'What's that?' He asks intrigued, with questioning raised eye brows, as one of the early-birds carries his rig past him to the beach.

'The down-haul's broken, and this was the only rope I had in the van, not ideal but it will do the job, won't need any fine adjustment today,' the early-bird nodded upwards and out to the sea to emphasise the conditions with a grin, 'I'll probably have to cut it off at the end of the day, but it will do the job and get me out on the water, that's the main thing.' Smiling a bit manically with a hint of nervousness, the early-bird continues with a sigh and a shrug to the beach.

He watches the early-birds launch and charge out into the waves and wind.

The storm shows no sympathy

Early-starters upended one after the other into the churning sea.

The wind howls…or is it Neptune laughing at their impudence, for defying him?

The green is now a jumble of preparation.

Shouted greetings.

Sounds of laughter.

Sails flapping madly.

All whipped away by the tireless wind.

Will their words be heard by others miles away downwind;

A whisper, an echo of this place and people?

Everyone is exchanging rig, sail and weather thoughts, tips and opinions accompanied by lots of watching of others on the water. All the while glancing and tutting at the darkening sky gathering up river over Canvey and heading this way with a vengeful look.

Suddenly everyone's ready. Carrying their rigs, the short walk from the green over the path, to the beach, being careful to mind the staring buffeted walkers and their wind ruffled dogs with rippling fur.

The waves pound the beach.

Seaweed thrown up on the tide line.

Sand blowing in the wind.

He can feel sand scraping his face,

He can taste the salt in the air with every breath.

Last check; rig all set,

wet suit all done up,

buoyancy vest and crash hat on.

Deep breath.

He takes a step into the water.

Glancing down he notices a plastic bottle and other detritus that turn his stomach

He makes a mental note to pick it up and put it in the bin when he comes back in.

Angry waves splash and bump him.

It doesn't feel cold, as he steps deeper into the water.

He feels the undertow push and pull him.

Ready to go.

He rises from the water onto his board taking off towards the pier end with everyone else.

Wind surfers skimming over and through the waves occasionally airborne as they launch off waves at breakneck speed.

Kite surfers, multi-coloured chutes, bright petals ballooning above them bringing the only colour and relief to the grey of the day. Skimming and at times lifting spectacularly into the wild air high above the frantic seas.

The hydro-foilers gather speed quickly then lift above the water, looking like some miracle as they effortlessly travel above the churning waves.

All on the edge.

Every sinew straining.

Hearts pumping.

Adrenalin rushing.

Absolute concentration.

All feeling so very alive!

The storms frantic turmoil surrounds them.

Always threatening to engulf them.

They race out into the gale.

Each cleaving their own white cloud of white water in their wake.

They whoop.

Shout.

Taunt each other.

Just more whispers lost in the storms roar.

Neptune is not so easily tamed; now the challenge is made. The wind and waves become more confused, catching out the unwary, any lapse in concentration is cruelly chastised with a violent dunking into the unforgiving sea.

On seeing the board in front of him fall in a spectacular misty explosion of water, he depowers as best he can and goes past to check the rider is OK. He is greeted with a hand in the air and a sodden smile as he slices by.

All OK.

He laughs.

He's going well.

The right sail.

The right board.

He believes he has the feel for the conditions,

The weather gods have other ideas...

Without warning, his rig somersaults forward and he lands face first with a deep splash, a green wet slap in the face and a more than a mouth-full of salty water to gargle. He splutters from the surprise water-boarding, gets his breath as he bobs about in the buffeting sea, gathering his thoughts.

Then he sees her rocketing towards him pulling a white wall of spray behind her. *Oh no,* he thinks as he sees her quickly getting nearer, then he sees her looking towards him through the swirling sea. She briefly raises one hand from the boom to wave, which he reciprocates.

He's OK.

She nods at him with a just discernible smile through the waves that splash over her and keep irritatingly slapping him about as he sits wallowing in the water. She then turns smoothly in a carved half circle round him and powers back towards the pier, both hands tightly back on the boom using all her strength and skill to tame the day. *Oh no, she's used me as a turning buoy,* drifts through his head as he struggles with the rig, the wind and waves bumping him about.

As he wallows, the sun makes a sudden appearance through a tear in the grey clouds. Honey coloured beams of light chase away the grey, white wake becomes sheets of liquid diamonds sparkling as they are whipped away by the wind. Sun beams refract through the water vapour throwing rainbows of colour in all directions. He can also feel a slight warmth in the air. With effort he finally manages a water start and he's off again. The sun vanishes as suddenly as it arrived, the storm redrawing its grey curtaining across the sky.

He accelerates furiously.

Everything blurring, flashing past him in a haze of wind and stinging spray.

He glances at the sky coming in, dark and threatening; more wind and probably rain.

He knows he's tiring, so he heads for the beach for a rest and to see what the incoming weather brings.

As he pulls his rig up the beach, he realises how much energy he has used; muscles aching, eyes stinging, still coughing occasionally from his force-fed seawater swallowing. He decides to take the rig back to the green. It's a bit of a fight with tired arms carrying it in the wind, but he lays the rig on the grass of the green with some relief, ensuring it's not going to fly away in the next angry gust.

Plodding.

Tired.

Back to the tideline

He picks up…

The plastic bottle,

and some

unpleasant sticky matted ugly coloured cloth-soaked wad.

Thank God for wet suit gloves.

His gag reflex makes him cough.
He takes them to the bin.

The dark cloud hurries in from the west, squally sheet rain arrives with a vengeance. He decides that's enough for today. The rain washes the salt water from him, he shivers involuntarily and retreats to his van to change before he gets colder. He can hear the wind howl and rain rattle on the van. As he peels off his wet suit and changes into dry clothes, he notices bruises emerging from his high-speed tumble. He can feel the van moving slightly in the wind again.

Changed he pulls open the van's sliding door and peers out, the rain has stopped and the dark cloud with its vengeful weather has passed and is hurrying off into the North Sea.

The wind is settling
The sea not so angry.
The tide has turned.
All a bit calmer.
But it's still grey.
No sign of the sun.
Shall I go out again?

'Do you want a cup of tea? I'm popping up to the cafe.' someone shouts at him as he stands on the green looking alternately at sea, sky and his rig laying on the ground wondering what to do.

'Yes please,' he answers.

'Cake?'

'Yes please,' he answers again .

Decision made, he knows he's tired and he feels a bit battered and bruised. So, he packs his kit up into the van and then loiters longer than he should, chatting and exchanging stories of the day while drinking tea and eating cake.

He joins others standing on the path looking out to sea.

ALL SAFE.

Everyone accounted for.
All back in one piece.
If a little battered, bruised
and tired.
But exhilarated and excited after such a wild day!
And there's always tomorrow.
Down to the sea again
It's in the blood!

(Acknowledgments: Thanks: Sonia, Andy, Doug, and Paul... the riders on the storm.)

INSERT COIN

ALEX DELVE

Rhys and Steve crouched in the midnight darkness outside the arcade and waited for the world to fall silent. Adventure Island was a scattering of skeletal silhouettes against the grey sky behind them, and glints of moonlight glimmered on the sea beyond.

"I don't like it," said Rhys, his voice a low rumble. "It's like the town is dead."

"Well," replied Steve, "we can come back in the morning and rob the place in broad daylight, if you'd rather." He pulled a key from his pocket. "Or we can get on with my plan as agreed."

"Where'd you get that from?" asked Rhys.

"Let's just say it's amazing what fifty quid and corruptible teenage staff can do when brought together."

He reached down and unlocked the padlock at the bottom of the arcade's shutter, before taking hold of it and nodding at Rhys to do the same.

"Slowly," he said, easing the heavy metal upwards, wincing at the screech it made. Once the space beneath was about waist high, Steve hissed at Rhys to stop, then ducked beneath and inside.

"Now you," he hissed. "Get a wriggle on."

Steve barely kept the shutter level as Rhys followed, and for a moment feared his arms would be ripped from his shoulders. Muscle was the only reason he needed Rhys at all; in a fairer world, where brains were properly rewarded, Steve would be out here on his own. And taking the whole payout too.

Steve's strength gave out and the shutter clattered to the floor.

"The fuck you do that for?" he hissed.

"I didn't do nothing," replied Rhys. "You had the weight."

"Whatever. Just get your torch on."

The darkness inside the arcade was so complete that when Steve raised his hand in front of his face he couldn't even see the outline. Then Rhys's torch burst into light and a horrific face, its distended flesh grey and falling from the skull in clumps, filled Steve's vision. He staggered back into the shutters, arms flailing around his hand.

"It's just House of the Dead," said Rhys, pointing at the garish red lettering beside the acrylic image of the zombie. "Completed the whole thing without losing a life."

Steve puffed out his cheeks, tried to ignore the hammering of his heart against his ribcage. "You could have warned me," he said, before rolling his shoulders like a boxer before a fight. "Right then. Let's see what we've got."

Rhys panned the light across the arcade, making shadows slip out from behind the cabinets like curious phantoms. A car, its engine noise deepened and amplified by what sounded like a ridiculous muffler, roared past and Steve flinched again, his body still soaked with adrenaline.

"Did you bring the drills?" he asked.

Rhys rummaged in his bag and produced two, passed one to Steve, who indicated a row of cabinets on the far left of the arcade. "You start there. They only empty them once a week so they should be full to the brim."

"On it,"

"Be quick. I want to be in the car and gone in twenty."

Rhys went, and took his torch with him. The light shrank and the darkness expanded, wrapping itself back around Steve. Feeling gooseflesh rising up his spine, he reached into his pocket for his phone, but his hands were still slick and shaking and he fumbled it. It cracked onto the thinly carpeted floor, then scuttled away into the darkness.

"Mate," he called, turning toward it. "I need a-"

The words died in his mouth. There was a square of light on the far side of the arcade, hovering in the dark. It flickered as though shining through gently rippling water.

"You need something?" called Rhys from where he was working. His drill whined between his words.

"No. Nothing. All good." Steve remembered the darkness when they'd entered, the totality of it. There was no way this cabinet had been switched on then, and neither he nor Rhys had been anywhere near it.

He approached it. Slowly, and with his pulse thudding in his throat.

Another boy racer careened past, and his time the sound made Steve jump a foot into the air. Rhys asked him if he was OK in a tone that would have earned him a slap had he been a foot and a half shorter.

The cabinet was little more than a wood and acrylic box, about a foot taller than he was, with a recessed screen about half way up and a panel with two joysticks about gut-high. The casing was the sickly green of florescent plastic. There was no name, no instructions, no words anywhere on the unit.

"What the..." muttered Steve as he leaned in to get a closer look. It was more modern art than video game; most of the screen was a black rectangle, framed by a bright, pixellated halo. Every few seconds, a grey shape would lance across the screen. There were no characters, no good guys or bad buys, no platforms and no guns.

"Rhys..." called Steve.

"Yeah?" Rhys turned to face Steve, and as he did so, the

black rectangle and grey lance flew away to the side, in perfect synchronicity. Now the screen just showed an off-green rectangle in the centre, and a shadowed shape beside it.

"Do me a favour," called Steve, trying to hold his voice steady. "Hold your hand in front of your face?"

"What? You going to slap it?"

"From here? Look, just do it, yeah?"

A hand emerged on the screen without a moment of lag.

"Thanks," he managed. Just. "You can get back to work now."

He heard Rhys mutter something, but he really didn't care what it was. He was trying to understand what the hell he was looking at. The room span around him and he grabbed the edges of the cabinet to steady himself, almost brushing the joysticks.

The joysticks.

The nausea in Steve's gut lurched with the thought of it. His hand shook as he reached out and laid his fingers on top of the left-most one. Player one. The pale light of the screen made his skin washed out and pallid. Sweat beaded along his hairline, and his shirt clung to him. The only sounds were of Rhys's drill, and of Steve's ragged breath.

He pushed the joystick to the right. A moment later Rhys was moving and it was all Steve could do not to scream. His hand leapt from the control and then Rhys was still again, features creased in confusion as though he'd fallen asleep and woken somewhere other than where he'd expected to.

"You alright there mate?" called Steve.

"Yeah," replied Rhys, looking at the barely-lit space around him. "Bloody mind wandered. Or something."

Steve drew a deep breath, then grasped the joystick again, moving Rhys in a small circle that took about seven seconds to complete. This time though, he was careful to place him back exactly where he'd started.

"Did you just stand up?" asked Steve.

"You what? No. Why?"

"No reason."

Rhys's drill fell silent. "Look," he said. "I know you're the boss an' all, but you've done a lot of talking and not much drilling. If you want to get out of here on time, then you've got to help."

Steve swallowed the words he wanted to say and the men worked wordlessly for the next few minutes, the sound of their drills punctuated only by the clatter of coins as they tumbled into the sacks. Another over-tuned car hared past, this time close enough for the shutter to rattle. Steve barely registered it; lost in a swirl of half-formed thoughts. Now it was his hands that moved as if controlled from elsewhere.

"What are you doing?" Rhys's voice, hard and loud, brought Steve back into the world.

"What do you mean what am I doing?" Steve turned and stood. Took half a step backwards so he didn't have to look up so sharply.

"Look down."

"Why should I do-"

"Look at your money bag," repeated Rhys, his voice firm.

Steve did so. His body was tense with anger and primed violence, his jaw clenched. How dare Rhys even think of-

All the hostility drained from him when he saw what Rhys had. Instead of the concentric gold and silver of pound coins, his bag was full of cheap looking bronze tokens, large and flimsy like a child's play money.

"Did you not notice?" asked Rhys.

"Of course I noticed." Steve's response was a reflex.

"Then why are you filling your bag with them rather than actual fucking money?"

It was a question to which there was no sane answer. Rhys waited a few seconds until it was clear Steve had no intention of offering one, then thrust his own money bag in Steve's face. It made a sound like chainmail as it moved, and even in the dim light it glinted like pirate treasure.

"You're an arrogant prick," said Rhys, lowering the bag.

"You think I'm too dense to notice how you talk to me, but I ain't. You think I'm good for nothing but hauling open doors and carrying the load like a fucking donkey.

"Well I've got a sack full of cash, and you've got a few handfuls of worthless token. So who's the clever bastard really?"

"We split the takings," replied Steve. "Fifty fifty. That was the deal. You wouldn't even be here if it wasn't for me."

"And without me, you'd be stood on the street freezing your nipples off. If you want this money - what I've earned - then take it from me."

Again, Rhys waited for Steve's response. And again, none was forthcoming. He turned away, headed for the exit.

"Fu-" he started, but Steve grabbed the joystick before Rhys could finish the expletive. The big man froze mid-stride, and Steve turned him around. His eyes were rolled back in his head, the lids flickering obscenely. His jaw was slack, and there was a limpness to his gait that hadn't been obvious at distance.

Steve's gut lurched, and it was all he could do not to vomit across the arcade floor.

He remembered the money bag that hung from Rhys's clenched fist barely a moment later. He eased the big man three steps forward, until he was just about in reach. Two more would have been more comfortable, but this was as close as Steve was able to get to Rhys's ventriloquist-dummy features without losing either his nerve or his dinner.

He prised Rhys's grip open just enough that he could grab the coins from the bag, then transferred them into his own, before replacing them with the worthless tokens he had gathered. Tension went through Steve's back and chest like a blade; there was nothing to suggest that, at any moment, Rhys wouldn't snap out of the hypnosis, or whatever the hell this was, and explode with anger.

All he had to do was to manoeuvre him back to where

he'd taken control, and Rhys wouldn't notice. Not until he go home, at least, and opened up his bag.

By which time, Steve would be in bloody Newcastle.

A sudden noise made him jump, his body jerking as if he'd been electrocuted.

"Fucking boy racers," he muttered, then froze as he realised he'd let go of the joystick. Rhys's eyes were wide, his skin white with shock. His whole body shook.

Steve grabbed the joystick and Rhys's features fell slack again. Steve stood in the aftermath, as still as his victim, and tried to think logically. Rhys had been awake for three seconds, if that. Barely long enough to register his consciousness, let alone see anything. And what had there been to see? Steve stood beside an arcade cabinet, a black cloth bag in his hand. Nothing more.

Nothing more.

Gripping the joystick in a fist now slick with sweat, tightly enough that his knuckles blanched, Steve guided Rhys back to where he'd been, then paused for a moment. Caught a breath he hadn't realised he'd lost.

Then Steve released the joystick.

Rhys came back to consciousness with a physical jerk. For a moment he didn't move, and Steve wondered if it hadn't worked, if he hadn't really returned. Then the big man rounded on him.

"What did you do?" he bellowed. The noise was like that of a bear.

"What do you mean, what did I do? I don't-"

"I saw it. In your eyes." Rhys's face was flushed red, and he grasped his money bag so tightly his whole arm trembled. "I was there, then I was..." he pointed with his fist, unclear as to whether he was explaining it to Steve or himself. "I had another blackout." He looked up. His eyes widened. "You did this!"

Rhys rushed forward, his free hand open and reaching for

Steve's throat, who could do nothing but flail his arms and close his eyes. Wait for violence.

Violence that didn't come.

He opened his eyes much slower than he had closed them. "Rhys?"

But Rhys no longer cared about him. He was staring at the arcade cabinet, the screen of which was now displaying itself in queasy colours and blocky, distorted shapes. Rhys moved his head slowly from side to side, watching as the display showed his field of vision back to him. His confounded features were reflected in the screen like a spectre.

And then he realised.

As soon as Steve saw, he leapt for the joystick, but Rhys was quicker and barred him with an arm. "Tell me what is happening!" he shouting, his voice echoing in the empty space.

Steve moved again for the joystick, and this time Rhys pushed him away with his other hand. He lost his balance and coins scattered across the floor. Steve fell to his knees to gather them up but he'd lost his bearings and he hit his head on the cabinet, turning the glinting coins into bursting fireworks.

He stopped when an American voice announced that Player Two had entered the game.

Both men stopped. Look at each other. Looked at the cabinet. Steve moved first, but again Rhys was quicker and stronger. Steve got a glimpse of Rhys's fingers closing around the joystick when-

-Steve was across the room, at least fifteen feet from where he'd been. His head thumped and his stomach roiled. Rhys's hand hovered over the second joystick. Even at this distance, Steve could see that it was trembling.

"Step away from it," said Steve. "You don't know what it can do."

Rhys shook his head. "You've been, what, controlling me? Like a video game character?" He looked down at the bag of tokens in his hand, then at the coins scattered across the floor. "You were stealing from me?"

"I was making it fair. I was-"

"You were stealing from me!"

Steve raised his arms in the air, puffed out his cheeks. "I'm a fucking thief. What did you expect?"

"Better," said Rhys. "From the man you think you are, I expected better."

Steve had nothing to say, not to that. So he chose action.

The world seemed to move in slow motion as he dived for the cabinet. There was a moment where his fingers brushed the very top of the joystick, but his momentum took him past it and he tumbled to the floor. The wind rushed from him and pain exploded in his side. Rhys hauled him back to his feet, threw him backwards into the cabinet. Steve swore, gasping for enough breath to do so. He fumbled behind his back for the joystick, for control, for anything that might help him.

He found it, grabbed hold, and knew that he had won.

Then Rhys, impossibly, stepped forward and punched him in the face. There was a moment where Steve realised it was the wrong joystick - the one that controlled him - and that they only worked one way. Then the force of the punch sent him tumbling to the side and he felt the joystick break like a dry twig. His senses dulled, as though he'd been plunged underwater, his breath caught halfway between his lungs and his lips. Everything was a blur, a murmur.

He couldn't move.

Steve was dimly aware of Rhys shaking him, yelling at him, but he couldn't feel a thing. Certainly couldn't respond. He saw the coins fall, though, as Rhys emptied the last of his bag barely a foot in front of him. They fell like silently and gracefully, like shards of moonlight. He forced every scrap of willpower into his hands, into his fingers, begging them to reach for the money, but they refused to obey.

Rhys spoke once more, not that Steve could hear, then walked away. He left the shutter wide open behind him, the faintest of early morning light bleeding through the gauze of Steve's vision. Then, minutes or hours or days later, it filled with blue light, then red light, then blue. The brightness of it burned Steve's eyes, but he couldn't close them. The pain was dry and relentless.

When a silhouette emerged from the flashing lights, Steve tried to tell them what Rhys had done, to scream that he needed help, but his lips and his tongue wouldn't move. Nor could he fight when they carried him away, to a cold, dark space barely big enough for him to raise his arms, had he even been able to. Steve tried to call and yell and whisper and cry, then tried to hold his own breath until the darkness was total, but he achieved nothing by silence and stillness. Even when they pulled him out and put him on a table and shone hot white light into his eyes. Even when he saw the blurred image of Rhys above him, nodding to the coroner, and confirming who he'd been.

Who he still was, and who he would be forever.

THE PIER, MS AND ME

KAY-ANNE SHEEN

"The pier is Southend, Southend is the pier."
Sir John Betjeman

The tide was out when we started the long walk to the end of the pier. You could see the wet, firm sand way below through the gaps between the planks. I didn't like it. What if I fell through? I knew it couldn't happen but it didn't stop me being scared. It was the same with open staircases.

Mummy wasn't scared, nor my little sister. I walked quickly, almost running. I didn't feel safe until we were over water. Then I was happy.

That's about all I remember of the pier as a child in the seventies. That and how long it was. Mummy had told me it was the longest pier in the world but I didn't really take it in. How could we have something that was a world record so close to home? World records happened in other places, not Essex. I thought all piers were long.

In my teens, a college day trip took us to Brighton. Being on a Travel and Tourism course, I'd heard lot about Brighton Pier. It was supposed to be busy and full of life, with shows, fairground rides, arcades and bright lights. I was looking forward to seeing it. Then I saw it.

"Is that it?" It was so short! It barely stretched anywhere. It wasn't a proper pier. Surely Piers were supposed to be long.

In my late teens and twenties, I moved away and went travelling. Then I changed direction and trained as a nurse. My first job on qualifying was in Berkshire. The job was OK but I hated living there because it was too much in the middle of the country. I needed to be near the coast.

I returned to Essex as I approached thirty because I wanted to be within easy reach of my grandparents, who were beginning to show their age. I found a job that I liked and it became my niche. I bought a flat in Southend and settled in.

The pier still held its magic. I took a slightly longer route to work every day so I could drive along the seafront. I loved living by the sea and seeing the long pier reach out to the deep water. Every time a friend came to stay, especially if they weren't from Essex, I told them "We have to go down the pier." I was keen to share my passion with them.

Maria and I were there one windy day in March. I was wearing a short, slightly flared, denim skirt. All that night I kept dreaming that a gust of wind had caught my skirt and blown me off the pier. Because my skirt was denim, the seawater made it heavy, dragging me under, and the Lifeboat launched from the pier head to rescue me. The dream stopped as I was hauled out. Then started again. I rarely dream and usually forget them when I wake. But this one was so vivid and so scary it imprinted in my brain.

I always visit the Lifeboat Shop. I once saw a Lifeboat dinghy bring a pale, exhausted girl to shore. I was still a young child at the time, and the image has never left me.

Southend is the busiest coastal RNLI station in the UK, something they're proud of. At high tide the sea kisses the promenade and on sunny days the river glows blue, giving the area a Mediterranean feel. Low tide reveals a vast expanse of dark sand with shallow pools of sea, tempting beachgoers to venture out for a walk.

But it's deceptive. The water creeps away from the shore then rushes back in.

"Most of our rescues are people on sandbanks cut off by the tide," a volunteer told me.

As the first decade of the 21st Century progressed, so did my MS (Multiple Sclerosis) which I had been diagnosed with in 1997. My walking distances became shorter and shorter, and my energy less and less. Walking along the pier was no longer an option but at least I could take the train.

There were two trains. One was called John Betjeman. I knew who he was. Born in 1906, he was Poet Laureate from 1974 until he died in 1984. The other was called William Heygate. Who's he? I asked one of the pier staff.

"I don't know," he said. He must have been new. I knew there was also a road in Southend called Heygate, but that's all. So I did my own investigation, and discovered some interesting local history.

Sir William Heygate was a former Mayor of London and first Baronet of Southend. He felt the town was missing out because steamers were unable to dock to pick up and drop off passengers because the water was too shallow, and they were going further up the coast instead. So he championed the idea of a pier. The plan received royal assent and the foundation stone was laid in 1829.

In 1890, an electric pier train began running, the first in the country. By 1929 the pier had extended to its present length of 1.3 miles making it the longest pier in the world. That was a title it held until a longer pier was created in 2006 in Progesso in Mexico. Even so, Southend remains the longest Pleasure Pier in the world with the longest pier railway.

By 1980, following a major fire in 1976, the pier structure had deteriorated and was in danger of closing. The council decided that it was too expensive to maintain. Outrage erupted in the local community and a campaign was launched to save it.

Sir John Betjeman, (not only poet laureate but creator and

President of the National Piers Association), joined the campaign and said the longest pier in the world was a national treasure. "You find yourself, when you've got to the end of it, at sea without being sick. You don't go up and down, you see. And the sea is quietly whispering around you."

It's true. Even when the pier is busy, there's a sense of calm about it. I was once at the end in misty weather when I could barely make out the shore as I looked back. It was surreal and mysterious, like being on an island in a faraway place. I loved it.

MS continued to march on until even taking the train to the end became difficult. There was only so near I could park the car before walking to the shore end station, and it was becoming not near enough.

Then MS fatigue decided that it was time to stop working. My energy levels improved. My walking did not.

The year before, my Auntie died and her little mobility scooter went to live in my cousin's garage.

"Do you want it?" she kept asking me.

"No. I'm alright. I don't need it." I kept saying. And that's what I believed. Determined to keep my independence, I persevered in my struggles.

I didn't want to go there. I didn't want to acknowledge that disability was forever creeping forward. I was still the person I had always been. The one who walked wherever she wanted. Using the train was OK, lots of people used the train. I could still walk.

I didn't see that a shrinking walking distance meant my world was shrinking. I lived in that bubble and in that bubble, I was independent.

I'm an independent woman. I don't need equipment to get about. I don't need help.

I was able to drive into town and park as close as possible, often on a double-yellow line with my Blue Disabled Badge, to the one shop I needed and walk there and back. One day, it didn't quite go according to plan. I knew I was pushing it distance wise but thought it would be ok.

But by the time I was three quarters of the way back, my legs felt like they wanted to give way on me. I could see the car and just before it, the chairs and tables outside a cafe. It was maybe another eight steps away. Surely I can make it. I wanted to hurry to get there quicker but couldn't. I was willing my legs along. Every step harder than the one before. With each pace the willpower needed to stop my legs folding beneath me increased. I have to make it, I have to get there. I wasn't aiming for the cafe. I was aiming for the seat. You can't crumple two steps from the cafe. Using every last ounce of willpower and determination, I collapsed into the chair. My legs gave up the effort.

I sat there for as long as I dared, trying to regain enough strength to walk the last couple of steps to the car, all the time hoping that the cafe owner didn't emerge and tell me to move on unless I ordered. After a few minutes I had enough strength to stand and make it into the car. Thank God my car has hand controls. My legs could rest all the way home.

That's the thing about MS, it takes over by stealth. You convince yourself it won't change anything, and in the beginning it doesn't very much. Relapses happen and you recover to almost, but not quite, where you were before. But each one chips away a bit more. And even in between there are almost imperceptible changes, so small you don't notice until you look back.

I wasn't looking back and I wasn't looking forward. I was living in the now. I could drive to the seafront, park the car and walk to the pier station. The joy of living by the sea was still there, beckoning me.

The problem was that I was having to go first thing in the morning before it got too busy in order to get a close enough space before the day-trippers arrived. I didn't want to have to get up earlier than I might otherwise have done in order to go in the morning. But I'm not a morning person.

I wanted to go down the pier when I wanted to go, not when parking space availability dictated. Then, even going early didn't get me near enough. I hate not being able to walk very far. It's not fair. It's horrible. Why did I have to get MS? It's ruining everything. Everything I wanted to do, I can't do now. Why did I have to stop working? My income has halved. My friends are all still working and not around in the daytime. What am I going to do?

I can't sit and vegetate in front of the telly. That would be too depressing and I would go mad. Two days in the house and I'm itching to get out. But I can't go anywhere much if I can't walk very far.

I could though, drive to a cafe and sit there. Maybe now's the time to start doing what Nan had suggested. "You should write a book about your travels," she had often said. So I invested in a little laptop that wasn't too heavy, drove to the Cliffs Pavilion, sat there with a coffee and a view and got started.

The pier was still calling to me though. I need to go down the pier. I have to go down the pier. How am I going to do that? There has to be a way. There has to be. I kept thinking. Thinking and thinking. Turning it over in my brain, going round in circles, getting more and more frustrated.

Then one day I had an idea.

Auntie Myra's scooter.

That scooter would allow me to go distances that were further than I could now walk. That's what independence was.

I rang Helen. "Do you still have your Mum's scooter?"

So I took the train to Norfolk and came back with my wheels. The scooter was old and worn out and I needed to get new batteries because the old ones were dead. But it worked, which was the important bit. It was small enough to be allowed on buses and came apart into four pieces to go in the boot of a car. It was too heavy for me to do that, but other people could. When my Motability car was due for renewal, I got one with a hoist that was big enough for it to be lifted into the boot. My world opened up again.

Scooter and I set off. As we passed through the pier entrance gate, excitement quietly built within me.

The pier stretched out before me. Through the cracks I can see the mud below, no longer scary. We made our way down the sloping walkway until we were running side by side with the train line coming up to meet us. We're committed now, I realised. We can't change our minds halfway and catch the train.

Leaving behind the screams from Adventure Island, I began to enjoy the calm, but after a short distance, I came to a stop. A group of primary school children in their uniforms were filling the walkway, all chattering and holding worksheets, their teachers following behind. "Excuse me!" I yelled. But they were engrossed in conversation. "Excuse me!" I yelled again, a bit louder. One of the girls turned to look and moved in a rush, pulling her friend with her. "Children, let the lady past," I heard the teacher say from behind me. Slowly, like a ripple, they moved to the side. "Thank you," I called as Scooter and I crept past.

I love hearing children laughing and enjoying themselves but I wanted to keep going. We resumed our quiet journey, over water now and approaching the first of four shelters, a welcome relief when it's windy. What seems a gentle breeze on the shore feels gale force on the pier. Not today. Today there is no wind at all. The sky is pure blue and the sun is hot.

I passed a couple with a small child as they stopped to take a photo. A seal popped its head up to say hello then disappeared in a blink. There's a colony of them living on a sandbank in the middle of the river. If you have binoculars and the tide is the right height, you can see them.

A signpost on the rail informed me I was a 1/3 of a mile from shore. Oh goodness. I'm not even halfway yet. Another shelter. This one had a fisherman casting his line.

"They're not biting today," he told me. "There's not enough wind to chop the water."

I stopped to look back towards the beach. Its length was becoming more visible. The people on it looked tiny. The couple with the small child ambled round me.

A train hummed past. Scooter and I continued, accompanied by the sound of waves lapping and seagulls squawking as they flew overhead. The smell of the salt water and fresh air was heady. I caught a snatch of conversation as an older couple strolled by on their way back to shore.

Another sign. 2/3 of a mile. I had forgotten just how long this pier is. The walk is neverending. Another shelter and another fisherman. Then another train. Well no. The same train going in the other direction.

I was still enjoying myself but, even going full speed at 4 mph, it felt a long way. I couldn't stop yet though. If I wanted a cup of tea, I needed to wait until I got to the end. We trundled on passing the couple with the small child again.

Another shelter and a bit further, another sign. 1 mile. Getting there. The end is in sight. I can see it looming.

I was both relieved and satisfied when I reached the Pier Head station. Beyond, the pier widens into a large area. The cafe for my much-needed cup of tea has a zigzag slope up the wide steps to get in. Scootering up it felt a bit precarious, especially at the U-turn bends and on my way down with my tea in my travel mug. Several of the wooden picnic tables on the pier deck had a number of people sitting at them. I found an empty one and positioned Scooter next to it. There are also black metal benches dotted around. And at the far end, the Lifeboat station.

John Betjeman was right in his assessment. I was definitely out at sea now. Southend seafront was tiny in the distance, too far away to make out any people now. Looking the other way, Kent was even further away. How wide is the river at this point, I wondered?

That was thirteen years ago and I've seen off three

scooters since then. My wheels are my legs and I give them a hard time. I take them everywhere. Up bumps, down bumps, uphill, downhill, on buses, trains and planes, uneven ground, grass, pavement, cobbles, roads sometimes, and in shops and cafes where I can. I do long walks and short walks. I've occasionally been stuck and needed rescuing by a kind stranger. There are more helpful people in the world than unkind.

My latest and fourth scooter has a battery that will take me thirty miles, is still small enough for bus travel and separates for car boots. I can go back to "walking" everywhere, like I used to before MS intervened.

But my favourite thing is scootering along the seafront and down the pier. I don't care that there's not a lot at the end. That's not the point.

THE GARRISON

C. ELLIS-BALLINGER

13th October 1919

Some say I went mad, that I was, you know, sick in the head and I lost touch with reality; war will do that to you. The savagery of it. It breaks you one way or another. But I'll tell you my story and you can decide for yourself.

It started as an evening like many before it. We'd escaped the Officers' Dinner as soon as we could. I hated those formal dinners. Since the Great War, I felt out of place but none more so than with those posh new Officers and their pretty wives in lace. Flushed faces, full of youth, innocence and carefree confidence. It made me sick.

"Will you hurry up," Private Picton said, as he took the last drag of his cigarette and flicked it to the floor.

"Alright, alright, keep ya hair on," I called out, as I quickly did up my fly. I'd been desperate for a slash. It was dark, with no one around, so I'd gone behind a bush next to The Clock Tower.

"He ain't got any hair to keep on." Private Digby ducked out of the way as Picton tried to cuff him up the back of the head. Picton's giant shoulders pulled across his uniform; he's at least a foot taller and wider than skinny Digby. I saw his jaw clench as I trotted to catch up, Digby limped beside me. There was a quiet, stillness in the air. The West Gate was locked for the night. The parade green behind us, so full of regimental soldiers this morning, now felt abandoned.

"Long way back?" Picton asked. We all nodded, none of us were in any hurry to go straight to the barracks. I had been stationed at Shoebury Garrison since returning home. I was a soldier, I didn't know what else to be, so I trained recruits, tested weapons. It passed the time. I looked at my feet as my boots made a satisfying crunch through the piles of autumn leaves on the pavement. It was freezing now the sun had gone down. I rubbed my arms, feeling chilled to the bone.

"How young were those new Lieutenants, eh?" Picton said, hands in pockets. "Straight out of school and still wet behind the ears, the lot of 'em. Bloody useless." He sniffed as I caught sight of the scar running down the side of his head, it was jagged and pink. A huge chunk of shrapnel had embedded itself in the side of his skull. Doctors couldn't understand how it didn't kill him. He was back at the front with me less than a month later.

"I know," Digby said, pointing his cane at me. "What do they know about being a soldier? Imagine them in the trenches, they wouldn't last five minutes." I got a sudden image of Private Young. How he had died in my arms, blood pouring out of his gaping mouth, like a fish. His shocked eyes stared unblinking at me. He'd only arrived the day before, fresh as a daisy, not a day older than 18 with a face smothered in spots. I shook my head, I was sick of the sight of Private Young.

"Not like us hardened bastards are they, eh?" Picton elbowed me, nearly sending me flying and shot a quick glare at Digby, who had been sent home before the Somme. He'd been shot in the leg but rumour got around that he'd shot himself to get a Blighty wound. His limp seemed to come and go. He always blamed the weather. He works in the office next to The Clock Tower now.

Something slammed loudly behind us and we all jumped out of our skin. Digby swore. I held my chest, my heart thumping. Picton had squatted down and covered his head. He stood up quickly, red-faced and fuming.

"What the bloody hell was that?" He shouted. I patted his shoulder but he roughly shrugged me off. He turned away as he lit a cigarette, his hands shaking.

"Look, it was that posh twat who slammed the stable door." Digby pointed to an Officer standing at the crossroads, looking frantically from side to side. "Let's go teach him a lesson, toot sweet." We bowled up behind him.

"Can we help you mate? I mean, Lieutenant, Sir?" Picton crossed his arms and stared down at him. I shoved my hands in my pockets and looked away. I suddenly wanted the warmth of the barracks. I'd had enough red wine at dinner that I might make it through the night without waking up screaming. I didn't want any of Picton's antics getting me all riled up.

"Why yes."

I spun round as I recognised Lieutenant Bainbridge's plummy voice. He was the Commandant's nephew. Rich as you like but with a face like a pitted potato. He was pulling himself up; he was a tall lad but still nothing compared to Picton "I've just been to check on my horse and I was certain that the Commandant's House was this way but now I'm not so sure in the dark. Only arrived this morning, you see. Still getting my bearings." He smiled at us with all the self-confidence that comes with inherited money. Picton was listening and nodding along, full of sympathy and politeness. Here we go. I shared a glance with Digby who sniggered. The Officer stared at him. Digby quickly looked serious and blew into his free hand, acting cold.

"Bit parky tonight, innit." He said as I nodded along and tried not to laugh.

"Why yes," Picton said, "I see your predicament precisely, Sir. Allow us to escort you." He gestured up the road with a slight bow. I sighed and followed, already dreading whatever idea had popped into Picton's thick skull. Whenever he went into Bill Sykes mode, it was never good.

"That's awfully kind of you fellows. Did you enjoy the meal? I found the food surprisingly edible." Bainbridge smiled with his hands behind his back like an old man taking his dog for a walk.

"Edible? All that posh muck was too rich for my tastes and way too much garlic." Digby looked away in disgust. The food had been bloody delicious and we had all gulped it down. Our stomachs were still adjusting to having decent hot meals. We never took them for granted.

"Quite right, way too much garlic," Bainbridge chuckled and pulled at the collar of his uniform revealing a spotty neck. "I say, that's one hell of a scar you have there." He pointed at Picton's face. Me and Digby tensed and looked away.

"The Somme," Picton replied, looking dead ahead as Bainbridge continued to stare, eyes aglow with awe.

"I bet you saw your fair share of action during the war. I bet you killed hundreds of Germans. I was too young to sign up, otherwise I would have been straight over there with you." Bainbridge pulled at his cap, looking away into the distance no doubt imagining himself valiantly leading the cavalry into battle.

"I'm sure you would, Sir, I'm sure you would," Picton said to his feet as he kicked at the leaves on the street.

"I lost my cousin at The Somme." Bainbridge muttered, "Fine fellow, damn shame." He strolled in big long strides, so sure of his place in the world.

"I lost two brothers." Digby replied, "Loos and Marne."

"Loos." I offered up. We all talked like that now. Just naming places where we'd lost our loved ones. My brother Harry had a fearsome reputation as a bare-knuckle boxer in Whitechapel, we all thought he'd come home full of stories of how many Germans he'd killed. Instead, he'd died in agony, poisoned by our own Gas. I was the skinny bookworm, it should have been me.

The Commandant's house was glowing in the darkness, full of light and warmth. "Now here's a bit of history for you. See them grassy mounds, across The Commandant's Park. Didn't you say Sarg, that they're Viking mounds?" Picton walked backwards winking at me. I knew what he was thinking. "Let's go take a look."

Our boots squelched in the grass as we strolled across the green. The huge oak trees were chock full of large black crows, watching us.

"I didn't know there was a Viking settlement here?" Bainbridge put his hand over his eyes to see better. Kinda pointless when it's dark.

"Yes. The Garrison was built during The Crimean War, but way way back, it was a Viking settlement. They're what's left of the fortifications." I said, pointing ahead.

I could smell the damp earth as we approached the mounds. "Legend has it, hundreds of years ago when all this was wild land, as far as the eye could see, a Viking Leader called Arkyn Wartooth landed here with a longboat full of mighty Viking warriors." I placed a foot on the mound, leaning forward as the others stopped to listen to my story. "Noting its strategic location, at the mouth of the Thames, he decided to claim the land and massacred almost everyone in the Anglo-Saxon settlement here. He brought his family and other farmers over from Denmark and made a Danish Camp. They lived in peace for many years, growing wheat, rearing pigs and fathering many children. Little did he know that a young Anglo-Saxon boy had escaped the massacre that day and was growing up into a powerful, vengeful man.

"One day, after many years of waiting and scheming, The Survivor finally managed to persuade the weak King of East Anglia to attack the Vikings. But the Vikings were ready and war hardy, they beat the Anglo-Saxons with ease and celebrated with much ale and singing into the night. But The

Survivor had planned for this, he'd hired a small band of mercenaries and they sat behind these very mounds and watched and waited. Once everyone was asleep in their huts, the mercenaries spread out and silently killed all the men and boys in their sleep. Arkyn Wartooth awoke to the sound of wailing women and with a sword at his throat. The Survivor told the Viking that all his men and male children were killed and his reign was over. All the women folk were now to be taken as slaves. But Arkyn Wartooth was surprisingly calm as he smiled at The Survivor. He closed his eyes and started chanting in his ancient language, getting louder and louder as the mercenaries backed away terrified. Arkyn Wartooth placed his hands on the earth and howled like a wolf, declaring this land blighted and cursing all the men for generations to come. 'None shall prosper here,' he roared as he stood up and towered over The Survivor who stumbled back. 'Now it is time for you to seal your fate.' The Survivor panicked and swung his sword, swiftly beheading the Viking. The lifeblood of the Viking seeped deep into the earth, sealing the ancient blood curse into the land forever. The Survivor proudly placed the Viking's head on a spike, right at the water's edge, to warn any future invaders trying to claim his land. The Survivor dismissed the curse from the heathen Viking, being a God-fearing, rational Saxon and all."

"Wait, were the Saxons Christian then?" Bainbridge looked at me.

"How the bloody hell should I know? Do you wanna hear the rest of the story or what?" I looked at him, shaking my head. No patience, these bloody kids. But he nodded along for me to continue.

"So, you can guess what I'm gonna say next, can't ya? That's right, The Survivor married but all the babies were born dead. Every single one of 'em. The weather turned too, it would not stop raining, day after day, week after week. That's how that lake was created. It ruined his crops till nothing was left but mud flats and marshland. Soon people started getting ill, dropping like flies they were. People left in droves, calling the land cursed. Then his wife got ill and died, till it was only him left here, alone. Apparently, he died screaming in his bed, saying the Viking had come back to claim him. He died begging for forgiveness." I paused for effect as they all stared at me. "Now, I don't know if any of this is true. But a lot of the lads at the barracks reckon they've seen this Viking Lord patrolling the beach at night, axe held over his shoulder, waiting for fresh Anglo-Saxon meat." Digby stared at me.

"Did more Anglo-Saxons come then?" Digby asked, mouth gaping.

"Did more Anglo-Saxons come? Yes, of course, they did, you pillock. We're Anglo-Saxons. We're in Essex, Saxon land for bloody centuries." I rolled my eyes as Picton sniggered and Bainbridge bounded up the top of the mound with all the obnoxious, effortlessness of youth.

Bainbridge looked around as Picton came up behind him. "Cracking view. Right, you are old chaps, best be off now, but thanks for the story, highly entertaining." Bainbridge stepped forward but tripped over Picton's outstretched foot. He crashed down, face first, with a sickening crack. He continued rolling down the mound, landing in a heap at the bottom.

I froze. Shit. Picton dashed down after him.

"Careful there, Sir." Picton heaved Bainbridge up to a seated position, grabbed his cap, dusted it off and handed it back to him. "You stumbled on a tree root. Hard to see them in the dark. Especially if you're not used to this terrain."

Black blood gushed out of Bainbridge's nose. He leaned his back against the mound as blood dripped continuously on the grass. I quickly handed him my hankie. A cold shiver went up my spine.

"What the bloody hell do you think you're playing at?" Bainbridge mumbled, holding his nose as he staggered to his feet. "I could have you court-marshalled for this."

"Whoa. Hang on there, you tripped. We all saw it. Didn't we, Sarg." Picton said as they all turned to look at me. I nodded along. I was grateful for the darkness as blood flooded up my neck and flushed my cheeks. I felt sick and light-headed. Bainbridge turned away and stormed off.

"Serves him right." Picton elbowed me sharply in the ribs as Digby sniggered.

"We showed that pansy eh? Although, he didn't seem particularly scared of your ghost story, Sarg. Couldn't you have added a bit more blood and guts?" Digby looked at me.

"Tell it yaself next time," I said as I lit a cigarette and walked off towards the barracks. I'd had enough of these two tonight.

"Don't be like that, Sarg, wait up." They came up behind me as Picton knocked off my cap.

Picton clapped me on the back and chuckled as we arrived at the barracks. We could hear laughter down by the beach. Weston and Turner were sitting on the sand with a bottle of wine. Deep fatigue hit me as I looked out over the mudflats. The water was creeping in with the tide. Picton grabbed Weston's cap as Digby threw stones at the seagulls. I suddenly wanted to be alone. I strolled up the beach away from their laughter and jeering. My feet sank into the sand. I sat with my back against a rock and watched the moonlight bounce off the rippled mud.

I must have nodded off. I woke up to the tide coming in, soaking my feet and ankles. I swore and quickly stood up, feeling dazed. It was pitch black and freezing. I shuffled along the small strip of beach left. I saw something move out of the corner of my eye. I squinted but there was nothing there. It was windy now but quiet. No squawking seagulls. Just the lapping of the waves and the wind smashing against my face. I continued up the beach and saw movement again. I could hear footsteps, slow and heavy in the sand, coming closer and closer.

"Hello?" I bellowed, "Is that you, Picton?" I looked from side to side but I couldn't see anyone. Crunch, crunch. Louder now as I frantically looked up and down the beach. Then I felt breath on the back of my neck, slow and heavy, with the stench of rotting flesh and mud. Just like the trenches. I spun around to find a huge man towering over me. His head was covered with a wolf's pelt. His haggard face dripped with blood that trickled down his long plaited beard. He fixed his pitch-black eyes on me.

Holding his axe high over his head, he howled and a blinding light shot out of his mouth. I stumbled backwards and blacked out.

I awoke with a start, my head pounding and my vision blurred. I felt a sticky, wet warmth soaking through my jacket. I struggled to sit up as my hands slipped on the wet grass. I was on top of the mound. How did I get back here? I could smell the coppery blood, I was smothered in it. I shot to my feet and looked around, rubbing my eyes and smearing blood on my face. There were two bodies on the green. I staggered down the mound and ran towards them, my heart thumping in my ears. One was Picton, his whole face and head had been completely smashed in. A few feet away was Digby, his legs had been hacked off. I staggered back, shaking my head. I could hear a whistle being blown. Lieutenant Bainbridge was running across the green in his check dressing gown and slippers like a Lord chasing away a poacher.

"What the...Dear God man, what happened?" He turned away from Picton and threw up. Bent over, hands on his knees, as he heaved.

I was suddenly knocked off my feet. I landed face-first in the grass as I felt a gun digging in between my shoulder blades.

"Don't move, you sick bastard," a voice shouted from behind me. I could see feet running in all directions as two more soldiers hauled me up. Neither of them looked at me as they began pulling me away.

"It'll never end," I said but no one was listening to me any more.

NO PLACE LIKE HOME

STEVEN ROSEN

An icy blast ripped the tattered lapels of the overcoat two sizes too large from his claw-like hands that had neither strength nor will to hang on. The wind whipped cold rain around his shrivelled frame, ballooning the back of the coat like a parachute and dragging him backwards. 'God, I hate you.' Spat the old man, wondering if God would hear through the howling storm lashing the clifftop of Belton Hills.

Clenching his fists, he thrust them deep into his pockets and wrapped the coat around himself as best he could. Touching the half-full glass bottle of golden liquid, warmth stirred in the depths of his gut. Looking to the distant estuary, the night met the raging waves, and he remembered.

A rising sadness engulfed him as despair sucked at the little strength that remained. It took all his will not to allow his legs to buckle, for he would surely end his days in the black of night on the cold, wet path.

My friend. A voice beckoned on the wind, and unsure if it was in his head, he looked up as rain seeped into a soaked collar. 'Yaaaa,' he mumbled as the cold wetness trickled down his back.

Raising his head, with slit-like eyes in a weather-beaten face, he scanned between the waves of sleeting rain. He focused uncertainly on a large shadowy figure barely distinguishable against the tall bushes and undergrowth that thrashed wildly before being pressed into the blackness of the night as if by a giant hand.

My friend. The voice beckoned.

His fist released momentarily before wrapping tightly around the bottle of scotch as he leaned his weight toward the direction of the voice and dragged one sodden leg after the other in a slow-motioned pantomime.

Head down and faintly aware of low branches whipping overhead, he fell blindly through his next steps, stumbled and lurched forward, but his outstretched hands connected with a robust and firm limb of the shadowy giant. 'Excuse me, I'm the worse for wear,' The old man said, straightening himself upright.

He turned with a drunken smile and a slight sway to the shadowy figure beside him. 'You've found good shelter here,' he said, leaning unintentionally onto his friend, who seemed not to mind. 'I'm so tired I just need to sit for a moment,' he said, sliding gently to the wet ground.

Taking out the bottle, he twisted the cap and threw a gulp down the back of his throat. The liquid felt warm as it glided down to heat an empty stomach.

Holding the bottle aloft, he waved it in an offering, but the half-hearted gesture was met by silence. Nodding to himself, he stared at the bottle and smiled.

It's not the storms that will kill you.

Sighing deeply, the warmth of his scotch-laden breath was both pleasing and revolting as a deeper voice from within drew his mind back to a time when Belton Hills was bathed in warmth, sunlight, and the laughter of a child as he chased his mother around the front garden of the large detached house in an Indian headdress with a bow and arrow set with red sucker pads for arrows tips.

Through the sleeting rain, he watched them with a smile that delivered a sharp, deep wave of loss. 'We all lived here, you know,' he said, gazing at the houses that overlooked the Estuary a few hundred meters away but undistinguishable through low visibility. 'Are you native here?'

I put down roots here many years ago. I have witnessed many changes on this hill.

'Me too, my friend. When I lost her, I gave up, you know. My son never bothered to make the trip from Australia for the funeral.'

A memory of the last time he saw his son flashed in his mind's eye. The last words he screamed at Jason before he stormed out of the house were bugger off, back to where you came from.

Jason had fixed him with a glare of anger, but underneath was the pain of a wounded boy. As the anger subsided, softening his face, it became a mask of pity. This is where I came from, Dad. They were the final words they ever exchanged.

Tears filled bloodshot eyes as he gulped hard and took a long swig from the bottle. He was self-righteous back then, thinking being the breadwinner – feeding, clothing and putting a roof over their heads was enough.

That belief was the foundation that steered the course of his life. *How did I get it so wrong?* He thought.

I have lost, too. I watched them fall at the hands of your kind.

'I know, my friend, I am truly sorry. I took it all for granted. Selfish. I was completely selfish. Your friends spoiled my view. Ha,' His single laugh held no humour. 'Ellen detested me for it.'

A gust of driving rain breached the shelter and blasted him from behind. He shifted closer to his friend, who seemed to sense his need and gathered to close the gap.

Her face shone before his unfocused eyes, and the regret that had etched a thousand deep grooves in his face ceased to torment him. 'She was always the voice of reason, of love. I always considered it a challenge, so I crushed that voice.'

He stared hard, and her face faded, replaced by the night. 'You are all I have got left, my friend.'

I bear no malice.

Surveying the emptiness, they were alone. Only maniacs or those without choice would weather such a storm.

In the solitariness of their bond, the man took a small sip from the bottle and reached an arm fondly around his companion. As he leaned his weight slightly, it was met with an unmoving solidness that reassured him.

"I'm glad you're here, old friend; you're the only one that never judged me."

A car's high-beam headlights swept across the darkness, momentarily reaching his face and exposing the pain and isolation as he huddled in the shelter of the only one who still listened.

Suddenly feeling the cold, he placed the bottle to one side and pulled the collars of the coat together.

Where does this end, John? How many storms do you have left?

Glancing at the bottle, he whispered, 'It's my penance. What else do I have?' Closing his eyes, his mind wandered in a fog of thoughts and images. Feelings of sadness, regret and guilt fermented with the warm alcohol in his stomach, and he squeezed his eyes tighter to contain a wave of nausea.

A loud crack from above drew him from the bitter-sweet place. Feeling the cold wind bite the skin of his face, he heard a large branch thrashing wildly high overhead.

Hoping it would crash down and crush his skull, he felt the shield of his big friend and heard his words. *Go home, John. There's nothing for you in the storm.*

Opening his eyes in response, the night was replaced with a vision from nearly fifty years before. The sun shone, and a smiling pregnant Ellen waited at the gate of the freshly painted house. He watched himself, briefcase in hand and felt the wave of love he had felt rush through him at the sight of her.

Nodding, in surrender, he felt the warmth emanate from his ancient companion, and leaning his weight for support, he pulled himself up, encircling a girth so wide the hug felt incomplete. Closing his eyes, he pressed the side of his face against the rough bark and felt a timeless rush transport him in a tunnel of warmth and peace. Smiling, he clung tighter and felt his own heart's energy lifting, warming and flowing back into the source that nourished him.

The rain lashed on the wind as bushes and branches thrashed, and in that moment of embrace, he understood something that he had never felt before. Life was everywhere, pulsating through the tree trunk he held, flowing from its roots and breathing through its leaves. It was in the wind, the rain, and the storm's energy.

It was within him, awakened and vibrant. *I have been asleep.* He thought.

With a bold inhale, he gathered himself and stepped from the shelter into the storm's wrath. The driving rain lashed him as he clung to his coat, one hand pressed in a pocket and the other clutching the lapels. With each step, he drew strength from the storm, laughing wildly; he was the storm.

Crossing the grass, he stepped into the road that separated the street from the cliff-top gardens and stopped midway. Looking up, he studied the house, and his mind's eye superimposed a freshly painted fascia over the peeling paint and decaying pebbledash.

Approaching the front gate, he gripped the rusting metal catch and, turning, pushed the gate firmly closed against the wind. A light shone from behind a small diamond-shaped opening in the curtains. Watching it, he approached the door, hesitated and with a sharp inhale, fished a key from his trouser pocket.

The familiar feeling of dread that silently awaited engulfed him. Pushing the door, it swung open, and a lamp illuminating the front room cast a shaft of dull light into the hall—the emptiness followed as his eyes adjusted.

Once more, dear John. He seemed to collapse into a void within himself as his shoulders hunched, and the weight of his arms drew him forward and down, curving his spine.

His drenched clothing formed a puddle on the wooden floor. He turned, resigned to his fate and purposefully closed the front door.

It began with the Great Storm of 1987, which had ravaged whole swathes of the country. It was a month after he had buried Ellen, and as he had watched from the safety of the front lounge, trees were bent in half, and some uprooted as branches and debris flew through the air.

He had been drinking heavily since the funeral, and the pride that had cost him so much had turned inward into self-pity.

He had never learned to process any of the losses in his life. Never cried when his mother or father died, and didn't know what to do with the awful feelings that arose after he hounded Jason from the house for the final time.

Ellen's pleas for him to back down and reach out were met with a sternness that belonged in the Victorian era. She had often said he was born to the wrong generation.

As he lifted the white Mackintosh coat from the hall coat stand that night, he intended to head out to be claimed by the storm. After several hours, exhausted and beaten, he had taken shelter under the great oak opposite his house and waited for it to collapse onto him.

After drifting off, he awoke as twisted as a remnant of the storm wreckage and limped home. His hollow look and ghostly gait caused a neighbour to stop and watch him silently pass.

The despair was unbearable, and as he took the key for the gun cabinet his soaked and soiled clothing was hung as a last act of love in Ellen's wardrobe before he joined her.

Unable to fulfil his quest, the passing years saw his stature and presence diminished, and the clothing he retrieved only for great storms was now as tattered as his broken spirit.

As John headed along the hall to the kitchen, he stopped where the light from the lounge illuminated the faded photo of Jason chasing Ellen with the bow and arrow in the front garden.

A deep longing rose through the layers that had firmly held his emotions entombed. Tears dropped heavily from blurry eyes. He wiped them away, but they continued accompanied by deep sobs from his chest.

Focused on the fading glimpse of happiness captured behind a dusty glass film, he longed to escape.

This isn't part of the ritual.

His grief refused to be repressed any longer. *Why? Why John, Why?*

Thin, bony shoulders spasmed as he bore the release so long denied. The streaming tears felt warm and nourishing on his skin and spread to his cheeks, releasing the tension that dropped from his jaw.

'Oh, John.' His voice trembled with compassion and forgiveness. 'You have suffered many storms. It's time.'

Gathering what little strength remained, he shook his head violently from side to side, dispelling tears that flew in all directions. Ritually, he lifted the gun case key from the shelf and headed upstairs, leaving a trail of wet footprints.

Pausing at the top of the staircase, he stared longingly down the hall at Jason's door, which had been unopened for years. His pulse quickened as he looked at the cupboard with the gun case. Turning away, he reached for the Bakelite door handle of Ellen's room. With a twist, he pushed open the door and stared.

Ellen had withdrawn as her illness progressed to the room that had become her sanctuary. As memories flooded back, it resembled a museum of a previous life and the place where his desire for an end was at its strongest.

It has to end, John.

His eyes slowly swept the room, taking in the faded hand-embroidered bedspread they had once both slept beneath. His gaze reached the dressing table and focused on the painted porcelain hairbrush where strands of her hair were still entangled in the bristles. A deep sob jumped from his chest.

The loss he could no longer live with or hide from saturated the wasted muscles of his chest. Tears welled and warmly trickled down his cheeks as he smiled at a memory of Ellen smiling bravely up at him from the bed as he lovingly served her a bowl of barley soup on a tray.

Shaking his head, he said, 'This must end here, John.'

Breaking the ritual, he gently closed the door and walked along the hall. Ignoring the gun cupboard, he entered the bathroom and twisted the old-fashioned brass taps in the bathtub until they groaned, hissed and gushed out cascades of water, quickly filling the bath.

Stripping off the wet clothes, he folded them into a neat pile on the floor. Shutting off the taps, he climbed slowly into the bath and sank deep so the water gently lapped at his top lip. Closing his eyes, he thought *no more, John.*

Southend Council had been quick to react to the clear-up operation, and a gardening team was already at work with chainsaws cutting up fallen branches blocking the path and one set of the steps leading to the station.

Many people had ventured out, some walking dogs or travelling to work. Some had come to survey the storm damage. A window cleaner with a reach and wash pole was busy cleaning the house next door to John, while an estate agent leafleteer had just popped a free valuation leaflet through John's letterbox.

'I'd leave that one, mate,' The window cleaner said to the leafleteer as he worked on the small window directly above the street door. Then, a movement in the front window of the neighbouring house caught his eye.

Suddenly, the curtains he had never seen open in six years were drawn back. A man stared across the road, and the window cleaner followed his gaze to the large Oak tree battered by the storm with several large branches snapped and dangling, but the tree stood tall, swaying gently in the wind.

Looking back at the house, the old man was grinning from behind the dirty windows. He turned to look at the window cleaner, smiled and nodded.

John felt nourished after the best night's sleep he had had for as long as he could remember.

The pile of wet clothes were in a black refuse bag, and as John opened the front door to put them in the outside rubbish bin, he noticed the leaflet and stooped to pick it up. Reading it, he marvelled and shook his head at the photos of nearby houses like his with million pound price tags and red sold signs stamped on the pictures.

Looking over to the tree, he held up the black bag, waved it triumphantly and thought, *I'll not need these anymore, old friend.*

The window cleaner was delighted when John asked for his windows to be cleaned.

Sitting at the kitchen table, John stared at the finger dial on the old-fashioned telephone in front of him with the ridiculously long lead. He smiled, thinking how Ellen had refused to have a new socket fitted in the kitchen despite always sitting there in her favourite spot while on the phone.

Lifting the receiver, he reached out a finger to dial and hesitated as his eyes fell upon the leaflet. *His inheritance will compensate for all my failings.* His thought guided a disembodied hand to return the receiver to its cradle for a thousandth time, but a louder voice echoed from within. *John, there's no place like home.*

Lifting the receiver to his ear, he dialled the code for

Australia, followed by Jason's number. *It's been so long. I wonder if he is still there.* John's heart pounded faster and louder as the line rang, and his throat went dry.

The ringing stopped, and there was a silent pause.

'Hello, Dad.'

GHOST ON THE PIER

CATHERINE THORNTON

On the pier, if the moonlight gleams,
A ghostly figure haunts his dreams,
A spectral form in the dead of night,
draped in mist, a shimmering sight.

With tattered dress and hollow eyes,
This apparition softly cries.
Its voice a whisper in the breeze,
A tale of sorrow, and unease.

He once knew her flesh and bone,
now she's trapped in realms unknown,
her ghostly figure on the pier,
lost in time, forever here.

It wanders where the waves embrace,
searching for his long-lost face,
a love that's vanished with the tide,
in ocean depths, she'll now reside.

. . .

As the deep fog rolls in from the sea,
The ghost lingers, mournful yet free,
A presence on this pier of yore,
A haunting tale of love and more.

So if you stroll by the water's edge,
On that ancient, creaking ledge,
Beware the ghost upon the pier,
Whose story echoes, crystal clear.

PETER PAN NEVER GREW UP

BELLE HARPER

Everyone knew that if you went to the abandoned theme park - the one on the coast opposite the high street - on September 1st, the last night of the summer, you would see ghosts.

Ellie didn't believe in ghosts. She was fifteen, and so incredibly mature that she had no time for the hocus pocus bogus her mum spouted. Her tales of mornings spent queuing for entry wristbands, evenings spent watching the outlines of different rides light up in ludicrous colours, entire weekends spent on attractions - meant nothing. A fateful fire had left it abandoned for decades.

Nevertheless, armed with undersaturated polaroids, she would tell Ellie about the gleeful squeals that carried on the ocean breeze, describe in meticulous detail the American diner that made their poor waitresses sing to the Southend public. She spoke of great steep drops and large metal claws that spun around and around until yesterday's lunch churned up your throat; she described the queues in the summer and the emptiness under the grey, drizzling clouds of early spring. All the while, Ellie's dad would stand behind her mum with a sappy smile that was absolutely revolting to her teenage self.

A part of Ellie appreciated the way in which her mother's

eyes shone when she reminisced. But the stories were of another lifetime too far from her own to hold the same value. When Ellie looked out of the backseat window, driving past the seafront, she didn't see vibrant colours, or hear unrestrained laughter, or feel a sense of community brought through the knowledge that it wasn't even a good theme park; but it was *their* theme park. She saw blistered concrete, sickly sun-bleached plastic, and salt-corroded metal beams jutting from unlikely places. It was a sad mimicry of a real theme park; with the gates chained shut since before she was born, roofs blackened and charred on top of derelict buildings, and scorched tracks peaking above the fence.

And after every anecdote came the ghost stories. The myths of the spirits of children enjoying their last night before the new school year; spectral roller coasters, phantasmic merry go rounds and ghostly candyfloss. It was the same stories, same conversation, every year since Ellie could remember.

"It's not really abandoned," her mother would say, as though she were stating fact not fiction, "it just caters to a different crowd now."

"What, the undead?" Ellie would joke.

"Not quite," her mother would laugh, leaning down as if to whisper a brilliant secret. "I like to think it's for the children who never grew up, it *is* Peter Pan's Playground after all."

Ellie thought that was awfully morbid.

One summer evening, Ellie interrupted her mother's stories. She was fifteen years old, empowered by a google search, and brimming with the teenage urge to derail a conversation with blunt questions.

"If no kids died when the park burned down, how's it full of the ghosts of kids that never got to grow up?"

Her mum gave her a soft smile. The incredibly infuriating 'adult smile' that parents do, that held all the promise of knowing but never adequately explaining.

"They're not the ghosts of dead kids, Ellie, they're the ghosts of the memories kids made there."

———

"Memories" Ellie scoffed, kicking a stray pebble, sending it skittering across the pavement. "How can a place be haunted with the ghosts of *memories*, that's so dumb."

"I think it's sweet." Lizzie didn't even look up, preoccupied with balancing along the sea wall, arms out at her sides like a tightrope walker.

"No, it's just dumb."

"Does it matter? Your mum's always so happy when she tells you about that place."

"It does though, because it means this whole dumb city is obsessed with not even a dumb ghost story, but a dumb *memory* story." Ellie was beginning to think she needed to expand her vocabulary.

It was the first of September, Ellie was four days from starting year eleven, and held nothing less than utter contempt for the undead of any kind. She was determined to prove something by going to the abandoned theme park with Lizzie, and finding absolutely zero ghosts. She wasn't sure what she was proving yet; that her mother was an idiot for believing this stuff? That the whole of Southend were collective idiots for believing it? That Ellie, at fifteen, was smarter than a population of one hundred and eighty thousand? Or was she trying to validate the glimmer of childhood wonder that wanted her mother's stories to be true?

The sky was overcast as twilight loomed on the horizon, to their right the sea slapped against the stoney beach, black water broke into grey foam, frothing on the shore like an animal with rabies. The burnt-out funfair stood just in front of them; a blue spiked fence converging in a chain link gate, secured with a padlock and chain. Above the gate, the words 'Peter Pan's Playground' hung in a welcoming arch. The orange outline was peeling, the 'y' was dangling limply in the wind and a few letters had been lost to the decades, making it read as 'Pe er Pa s Pl y oud' instead.

"How do we even get in?" Lizzie stared at the gate, only now realising their excursion required trespassing.

Ellie gave Lizzie a smug look, then stepped back and took a running jump at the fence. Her fingers gripped the links while her toes balanced precariously in the metal framing, she followed the diagonal angles of the beams and awkwardly manoeuvred herself over the top, dropping down the other side to meet Lizzie's eyes through the fence.

Lizzie crossed her arms, face blank.

"That was not as graceful as you think it was."

Like the mature young adult she was, Ellie didn't warrant the teasing with a response. However, she did pull a face and glare while Lizzie made her own way up and over.

In the semi-light of a late summer evening, the two girls stepped into another world. A post-armageddon, alternate universe you only see in movies. Weeds had begun to break through the concrete, dying-yellow and rigid. Sand scattered across empty spaces and gathered against the foundations of rides. They strolled through a waste land, watched by cartoon caricatures of sun-bleached dragons. The old ferris wheel was missing carts, empty links swayed in the wind like apocalyptic windchimes. Lizzie skirted the scorched marks on the concrete, dancing around them as if, forty years later, the ground was still hot. Ellie walked through them, leaving footprints in the soot.

They explored at a leisurely pace, peering into nooks and crannies, playing guessing games as to how different rides used to work and what different stalls used to sell.

"This would've been a great place to hang out this summer, we could've had a dystopian picnic or a doomsday brunch. Those teacups would have been a cute colour. These bumper cars must've been fun. I wonder how fast that helter skelter was." Lizzie commented on every detail they passed, her chatter drifted through the dusk, mingling with creaks and rustles to stave off Ellie's uneasiness.

Time dragged on and the sky dimmed, dark places got darker and street lamps flicked on behind the perimeter fence, too far away to provide useful light. Lizzie's rambles trailed off, her eyes glazed over and the bounce in her steps morphed into a half-hearted plod. They weaved through the attractions, ducking under dully coloured debris and operator boxes with collapsed roofs. By the time the sky was an inky blue, Ellie was convinced they'd checked the whole park twice over. Yet not a single ghost had appeared. No glimmers of ectoplasm, no distant wails, no giggling children. Not even the wisp of a willow.

"I give up." Ellie declared.

"Wanna go home?"

Lizzie perked up at the prospect of leaving. But Ellie hesitated, for all her whole-hearted disbelief, she couldn't control the sliver of hope that wilted within her. The small part of her that still clung to every word her mother told her. She quickly squashed the feeling under adolescent vindication.

"Sure, let's go. It's official, ghosts aren't real. The whole city is wrong. I'm always right."

They wandered back through the park towards the gate. Now their wonder and interest had faded, Ellie noticed the silver canisters, cigarette butts, crisp bags, bottles, cans and other substances that littered the ground. Remnants of teen gatherings and young rebellion seeped from every crack in the pavement. Peter Pan's had been abandoned for decades, but the site itself had not been forgotten, just enjoyed by youth in an alternative, less savoury manner. Ellie found the thought sweet in a twisted way. She remembered her mother's theory of the park catering to a different crowd – maybe she wasn't that far off.

Past the cartoon dragon and mere metres from the gate, a faint whirring echoed through the park. The sky was black and the moon peeked from behind murky clouds. The faintest of glows illuminated the gloom, bringing back into view coasters that had climbed too high in the sky and disappeared into the darkness. With the glow, the whirring grew louder. Ellie paused and turned slowly, scanning for the source.

Below the dilapidated helter skelter, a misty grey figure manifested from bending shadows. Ellie could still see red and white circus stripes through its translucent form. She grabbed Lizzie's arm, dragging her to her side and pointing toward the ethereal shape.

"Look! Look!" Ellie didn't know why she felt the need to whisper; perhaps it was a subconscious fear her voice would carry across the open space and tear through the ghost, dissipating it before it fully arrived.

"What the fuck?" Lizzie whispered. Still holding Ellie's hand, she pulled them both along in a strange crab walk. They scuttled into a ride operating box, once connected to decaying Viking longships that spun around a singed dragon - the creature's head melted and burned at the base. They hid in the box, surrounded by cobwebs. The window was cracked in a few places, fractures threading through the glass. Beyond their makeshift shelter, they watched the shadowy being.

It was a young girl, eight at the most, with a grey plaid pinafore and white collared shirt. Her ankle socks had a lace trim and her black shoes floated a few inches above the ground. She had dark hair braided into twin plaits, held by little grey bows.

Another ghost joined the little girl. An older woman, most likely between thirty and forty. She had the same dark hair, but twisted into a bun at the top of her head - loose strands framed her rounded face, disappearing into wisps of vapour. A white dress billowed around her ankles, flowing out of time with the wind that periodically swept through the park.

Once the first two ghosts appeared, it was as if a door had burst open from the other side. Families with toddlers ran toward rides, leaving no footprints in their wake. Teenagers in flares, jean shorts and denim mini skirts congregated near the larger coasters and arcade machines. Before her eyes, the missing pieces of the park rebuilt themselves out of nebulous fog condensing into shapes. Tracks reconstructed by smoke, faded words and cartoons redrawn in monochrome, the donut stand refilled with spectral food.

Ellie felt like she was watching an old film in black and white, as the park around her came to life with the dead. She could hear them too. Airy voices and giggles rose into the night, accompanied by the chugging of phantom motors and wheels on chains. Every noise sounded staticky, like it were filtered through a landline, or a seventies radio.

Lizzie was equally transfixed, jaw hanging open, eyes darting in their sockets where she was trying to take in as much detail as possible and sear the image into her skull. But, despite how much Ellie wanted to memorise every outfit, every sound, every face, her eyes always returned to the first woman and girl. The pair drifted through the park toward them, leaving the cover of the helter skelter - its slide now shiny and grey.

There was a recognition she couldn't yet place. The hair, the eyes, the light smile of the older woman screamed familiarity. Then the woman laughed at something her daughter said and Ellie felt her breath hitch. That laugh was her laugh - it was her mother's laugh. It was her *grandmother's* laugh. A high gentle cackle, and it clicked. The dark wavy bun she'd seen in a hundred faded polaroids, the same smile, now unmarred by wrinkles and time.

But her grandmother was alive, Ellie's mother was alive. They weren't this frozen-in-time version of themselves, a toddler and young mother. They were an old lady and her middle-aged daughter. The ghostly replicas stopped their approach toward Ellie. The child version of her mother tugged on her grandmother's hand and pointed toward a stall with striped awning, selling candy floss. Swiftly, the pair melded into the crowd of ghosts.

"This is *insane*" Lizzie was whispering too, fearful of breaking whatever delicate enchantment this place had.

"I just saw my mum and nan." Ellie continued to stare at the spot where the ghosts had been stood seconds before.

"How? They're not dead - oh my god- what if they died in the past - like - three hours since we left yours?!"

Ellie laughed and turned to her friend. "I'm ninety-nine percent sure my dad would have at least texted me if that had happened."

Lizzie looked a little guilty. "Very true."

"But, this means that my mum was right." Ellie looked back to the window, its cracks smoothed over by a colourless haze.

"These aren't ghosts, they're *memories*."

They sat there for who knows how long - watching the past enjoy itself, listening to the memories of a place that would never make new ones.

When the torch beam cut through the open square, the ghosts in its path dissipated. The fissure through the apparitions was so distinct, it jolted Ellie and Lizzie from their stupor. They could hear the footsteps, real and thunderous compared to the distilled noise of the ghosts. The torch beam began to oscillate like a lighthouse, every spectral essence the white light touched burst into mist. As suddenly as it came to life, the theme park dissolved into a heavy fog. From the fog emerged the outline of a man, a torch in his left hand and a high-vis jacket around his torso. 'Security guard' reflected on his chest under the moonlight.

"Shit!" Ellie ducked down back into their operating box. Lizzie was a deer in headlights, the whiplash of events scattering her thoughts.

"Come on Liz, move your arse!"

They stayed close to the ground, ducking behind bins and wreckage that had been ghostly bumper cars moments ago. They moved quickly, relying on the background clamour of the seafront: cars, restaurants, wind and waves - distant, yet loud enough to cover their heavy breathing and hurried steps.

The gate wasn't far, and the guard had left the chain unlocked. Ellie crept towards the towering metal frame and pulled gingerly.

CRRR EEEEAAAA KKKKKK

"*Fuck.*" Lizzie cursed.

The torchlight whipped to them, they both stayed facing the gate, feeling the gaze on their backs, watching their own shadows mix with the chainlinks.

"OI! You two!" The voice was deep, scratchy and unmistakably pissed off.

"Run!" Ellie hissed, yanking the gate the rest of the way. It screeched shrilly but Ellie didn't have time to care. She sprinted down the pavement parallel to the sea wall, willing herself faster and faster. She heard Lizzie's wheezes behind her and, further down, the heavy pounding of their pursuer. She legged it until her lungs began to burn; she never had the best stamina and was well aware her escape was unlikely. They reached the pier entrance, the modern building jutting out into the path, swerving around it, she seized her chance.

She hopped over the sea wall, gesturing at Lizzie to follow. Together they slumped down, backs pressed to the wall, breaths held. The footsteps stormed past. They doubled back along the beach, passing under the pier and only emerging onto the concrete at the crossing. They jogged back up to the high street in silence.

It wasn't until they reached the top of the stairs that scaled the ridge of hills separating the upper and lower seafront, that Lizzie burst out laughing. Ellie soon followed with her own cackle. They must've looked ridiculous, two teenage girls, panting and sweaty, struggling to catch their breath between fits of giggles.

"If we do this again next year, we need to take up cross-country," Lizzie joshed.

Ellie wasn't focused on her fitness levels in that instant.

Her mind travelled back to the ghosts, the *memories,* the sheer number of them, the spectres of her own family, the magic of it all.

Peter Pan's Playground was small, burned and broken. But everyone knew that if you went to the abandoned theme park - the one on the coast opposite the high street - on September 1st, the last night of the summer, you would see ghosts.

GOOD WIND

ABIGAIL KEYS

The weather is uncharacteristically cold for an August evening in 1865. There hasn't been a blue sky in weeks by the time The Endor arrives in Leigh-on-Sea. Day turns to night with barely a flicker of light as Sarah looks down on the Estuary from her usual spot on Leigh Hill. She shivers, drawing her shawl around her shoulders as she scans the fishing boats scattered like toys on the water. They are impressive vessels, no larger than 50 feet, housing a handful of crew and boasting deep red sails the colour of mulled wine. As the boats pass, Sarah closes her eyes, picturing the image of her beloved on the waters below. It won't be long now she tells herself. Suddenly a familiar ship slides into view. It eclipses the other ships as it cuts through the water with a majestic ease, its sails blowing elegantly in the wind. Sarah recognises The Endor immediately, prompting her to sprint rapidly towards the dock.

She arrives just in time. A handful of other fishermen's wives have also gathered as the hull of the ship bashes gently into the rough faded cobbles. One by one their husbands disembark, and the couples slip off into the late evening glow. As the light begins to fade, Sarah realises that she is alone.

Doing her best to maintain her balance, she begins to climb the old weather-worn gangway.

The maternal rocking of the ship does little to stop Peter's stomach from churning. His face turns an unnatural shade of green, as he launches himself towards a wooden bucket across the cabin. It doesn't take long for him to bring up what little food he had managed to eat the day prior. Peter can't help but think that the manky slops almost tasted better coming out than they did going in. Slumping himself down beside his rickety cabin bed, Peter inspects the wound on his leg. It has formed an alpine range of gelatinous yellow pustules which encircle a deep trench of fibrous red flesh. Witnessing this only adds to Peter's growing sickness. In search of some comfort, he reaches into his pocket and pulls out a long strip of cream ribbon. He runs his thumb along the twists, caressing each knot in the fabric. Images of Sarah dance in his mind. It won't be long now he tells himself.

Suddenly Peter feels a warm fleshy sensation engulf him. As he raises his head, he wonders if he must be dreaming. Two eyes peer down at him, sparkling like the sun on the crest of a wave, as a hand gently touches his face. His skin is dry, sore and incredibly pale for a deckhand.

"Look at you." Sarah stares at Peter intensely, her golden ringlets bouncing around her face. She is an attractive woman, albeit in an unconventional way. Her face flushes a peony pink giving an innocence to her otherwise wild appearance. Her petite frame is adorned with an abundance of petticoats in various whimsical patterns. A thin leather belt twines around her waist, containing a variety of obscure objects; some small lengths of string, a sprig of sage, a red velvet pouch containing talismans from around the town.

"What happened?" Sarah rips a strip of fabric from her skirts, and dabs at the weeping hole.

"We hit some rough waters..." Peter winces as she attempts to clean the wound. Sarah stops and rests a gentle hand on his stomach as she waits for the pain to subside. The soft rise and fall of his breath, like an approaching tide, feels comforting and familiar.

"Are you here alone?"

Peter nods. The crew's fear of his infection and their annoyance at his subsequent idleness had not made him very popular in recent weeks. Sarah's cheeks flush in anger.

The next few minutes are spent tending to Peter's leg. Sarah gently dresses the wound with the last remains of fresh water on the ship, as despite her best efforts, she cannot find a single drop of alcohol to sterilise it. Peter watches her with loving eyes. Had she not found him here, Lord knows what he would have done. But Sarah had always been good in that way. In spite of what the town thought of her, to him, she had always been gentle and kind. He leans over and plants a small kiss on her forehead as she works. She smiles gently, fastening the makeshift bandage to his leg with a pin from her hair. A stray golden curl falls, landing beside her jaw.

"Let's get you out of here." Sarah hoists Peter's arm around her petite shoulder. Despite her size, she is unusually strong.

The vertigo hits from the moment Peter raises his head. He is barely able to take a few steps before the pair find their paths blocked by a burly shadow. Peter unfurls his hunched body just enough to make out the formidable silhouette of his Captain. Peter has never been particularly fond of the Captain. He has all the appeal of a rotten onion. His goose fat hair clings limply to his face as his yellowing eyes bear down onto the duo. He reaches out his hand, his fingers like chargrilled sausages, and gives Peter a hearty slap on the back. Thin lips emerge behind a thicket of greying beard, forming a disingenuous smile."Good to see you up and about hey lad. I'm sure a nice little spell on land will sort you right out." The Captain's lips curl upward, revealing little stubs of coal protruding from his gums. Peter had seen more teeth in a newborn. The Captain's gaze turns to Sarah. Although they had never been properly acquainted, the

Captain had seen Sarah a few times before, and he always felt uneasy in her company. Knowledge of Sarah's power was commonplace in these parts. For many years, Sarah has been the foremost vendor of charms, tarot readings and potions in Leigh-On-Sea. But what she was revered for was her 'Good Wind', which had become a tradition amongst sailors in the South East, for those who believe in that sort of thing. Good Wind consists of a piece of string or ribbon with a varying number of knots, and should a sailor find themselves in an unfortunate situation, one could simply release the knots and the wind would increase. The Captain has never been a big believer in such practices, but even he could not deny there was something a little strange about Sarah.

With Peter out of action, Sarah attempts to increase her business by trading closer to the dock. She busies herself behind a small stall adorned with a red embroidered cloth. It is strewn with cold brews of dried leaves in delicately decorated teacups, pestles and mortars of crushed herbs and spices, and tiny hand-printed wooden runes thrown in precarious patterns across the surface. The stale watery smell of the dockyard is transformed by the burning of incense, a rich spiced flavour perverting the air. Sarah packs her remaining belongings as business winds down for the day. In the shadows, Sarah can see a large, limping lump of a man emerging from the dusky harbour. She recognises the Captain almost immediately. The hairs on the back of his grimy neck stand up as he meets Sarah's gaze across the path. She never breaks eye contact as he approaches.

"Well, what have we here?"

"I was actually just leaving for the day." Sarah's tone is direct as she continues to collect her ribbons and glass vials.

"You read cards?" A deck of Tarot remains face up on the

table, the Lovers staring up at the Captain as he rummages around in a leather pouch around his waist.

"I would very much like to hear." A gold coin smacks down on the table. In no position to turn down business, Sarah lowers her belongings and sits down on a small wooden stool, beckoning to the Captain to do the same.

She can feel the Captain's eyes bearing down on her as she tosses the deck in her hand. Channelling the energy of the Tarot, she draws four cards, placing them face down in a diamond pattern on the table between them. The Captain never blinks. Instead an increasing interest grows in his eyes as Sarah reveals the first card, the King of Swords.

"Interesting," she mutters. Everything Sarah could possibly need to know about the Captain could be told from these miniature illustrations.

"I trust Peter is feeling better?" The Captain's eyes are anchored to Sarah as she flips the next card; the Ten of Swords. Sarah bites her tongue to prevent herself from replying cattily. The silence clouds the air like a thick fog. The Captain leans back in the tiny chair and runs his sunburnt hand through his scraggly beard. For a second, Sarah could have sworn she saw something crawl out of it.

"Terrible shame what happened to that boy."

"Terrible shame?" Sarah picks up the third card with a flourish. "He can hardly walk! He has an infection in his leg, he has been vomiting for days and the best you can do is terrible shame?" Sarah slams the card down on the table with more force than she realised she possesses. The Nine of Cups.

"What would you have liked me to do, Miss... Moore is it?" Sarah nods. The dim evening glow reflects off the water, creating a foreboding peacefulness around the dock.

"There's plenty you could have done." Sarah attempts to keep her voice even, but her frustration flickers out like a serpent's tongue. The Captain rises steadily like the burning sun, his tall frame looming over Sarah. Instinctively Sarah rises from her chair and backs away slightly, but the Captain is deceptively quick for his age. He snakes his hand suggestively around her waist pulling her close to him. His smell makes Sarah gag.

"And how do you know what I could have done? Were you there? Stowing away below the decks perhaps?" The Captain fingers the blonde curls around Sarah's face, the wistful lusting in his voice lingering in the air.

"Anything would have been better than leaving him" Sarah's body tenses with every movement the Captain makes. Her uneasiness does little to dissuade the Captain however, as he moves his hand away from her hair, past the nape of her neck and around the collar of her blouse. Almost without meaning to, Sarah's hand grabs at the Captain's arm, the pressure inside her body erupting through her fingers and pressing deep into the skin on his scraggly blackened wrist. The Captain is taken aback, relinquishing his hand from her dress to examine the four crescent imprints now tinted with blood on his wrist. A silence lingers in the air once more. Neither one moves for what feels like an eternity. He looks deep into her eyes, planning his next move, but to his surprise, Sarah stares right back, her eyes like the ocean, deep and unforgiving. As quickly as he had arrived, the Captain backs away and walks back down the street. Sarah breathes a sigh of relief as she stares down at the quadruplet of cards strewn across the table before her.

The Captain makes his way back towards The Endor, his thunderous footsteps alerting every passerby to his presence. He heaves himself up on the gangway where he finds many of his crew laughing and drinking. Still enraged, the Captain makes his way across the boat. As he does, he grabs the arm of a young deckhand who is emerging from below with two generous bottles of rum. Holding the deckhand in a vice- like grip, the Captain leans in close and growls.

"Nobody is to make any dealings with the witch Sarah Moore, and any who do so will be banished from the crew. Understood?"

The deckhand looks up at the Captain, surprised by the randomness of his command and the aggression in his voice. Curious, but unwilling to pry, the deckhand simply replies, "Right you are, Captain".

The weeks that follow are miserable. Business slows more each day; even those with no dealings at the docks make Sarah a pariah and she can feel herself coming to her wits end.

The morning of the ship's departure Sarah can barely console herself. She makes her way along the dock with Peter in tow. The early morning fog crawls out from the water's edge, nipping at her ankles like a rabid dog. There is an unfamiliar unease amongst the workers this morning. Their avoidance is purposeful and Sarah catches no more than an awkward side-eye from a young lad stacking traps. The rhythmic dragging of Peter's stick across the cobbles only adds to the tension. As she approaches the familiar hull of The Endor, Sarah stops short. She can smell the lingering odour of dried sweat and rum. As if on cue, the Captain peers down over the bow of the ship.

"You aren't welcome here, witch," the Captain scowls, "unless of course you have come to change your mind." This last part was whispered so softly that Peter did not seem to notice. Somehow the Captain had made these words only for her.

"I have come to say goodbye."

The Captain shrugs nonchalantly and turns back to his crew, continuing to bark orders.

Peter glances across at Sarah. He is beginning to look more like his old self again. Sarah gently flicks his hair away from his face, her hand lingering at his temple. Peter's eyes catch the light of the morning sun rising over the estuary. Fiery embers of gold and orange dance across his irises.

"Peter!" a harsh bark sounds from the deck.

"I have to go." Peter takes Sarah's hand from his face.

"I don't want you-"

"Sarah, we've been through this. I don't have a choice. We need the money." Sarah saddens as the truth of his words sinks in.

"Here," Sarah presses a thin length of blue ribbon into Peter's hand.

"I can't. If he sees it -" Peter curls Sarah's hand back around the ribbon. "Keep it safe for me."

"Please" Sarah pleads, but Peter's hand slips away. The scuffling of his walking stick grows smaller in the distance.

"How unfortunate." Sarah feels the Captain's beard tickle her cheek as he speaks.

She hadn't noticed him come down off the boat.

"This whole hopeless situation could have been avoided. Who knows what will happen to him now?" The Captain wraps his hand around Sarah's waist, fiddling with the ties at the back of her corset.

"If you hurt him -"

The Captain releases Sarah with a laugh."What will you do, witch?"

Fire flows through Sarah's veins as she storms back up the hill towards Broadway. Over the tops of the buildings she can see the ship move out towards the open ocean. The fire turns to acid rain as Sarah begins to weep. Collapsing to the ground amongst her dirty petticoats, she allows her tears to flow. As she wipes them away, Sarah realises she is still holding Peter's Good Wind. She runs her thumb over the silky fabric, the tiny knots entwined around themselves in a simple weaving. The knots in Sarah's stomach tighten as she recalls recent events in her head. The image of the Captain flashes before her. His grimy hands wrapping around her waist, barbed wire beard scraping her cheek, alcoholic breath invading her senses. All of a sudden, Sarah can feel her sadness subsiding.

The last remaining strings tethering her to logic and reason, snap. With the image of the Captain still tormenting her mind, Sarah holds the Good Wind out towards the silhouette of the passing ship. With an experienced elegance, she tugs at the knot. As soon as the final strand passes through the loop, the winds shift. The clouds knit together in a gloomy patchwork as Sarah's blonde curls fight around her face. The once tranquil ships are now hurtling across the waves. The Captain's voice plays repeatedly in Sarah's head. Cries of *'terrible shame'* and *'you aren't welcome here witch'* echo in the caves of her mind. A chill rises from the water as Sarah unloops the second knot. Fat droplets of rain begin to fall immediately as the sky becomes stained with grey blotches. The ships launch over the growing waves as they crash against the dock sending every boat in the estuary sky rocketing. Sarah stands in the heart of the storm. As she looks down at the chaos she is causing, she experiences no guilt. Not until the image in her mind changes to Peter. In her blindness, Sarah had not considered Peter. Instantly, her pulse raises. A bitter taste forms in her mouth and her fingertips pulse as if a surge of electricity is flowing through her. Panicking, Sarah scrambles helplessly, but she can no longer control the growing winds which encompass her. The last strands of fabric slip from their binding and the third knot is released.

Lightning strikes the top of the Broadway. Peter looks up in the direction of the light, a sinking feeling developing in the pit of his stomach.

"Secure the rigging!" The Captain barks orders to the crew frantically scrambling across the deck as the sky erupts into a thunderous applause. Peter can taste the salt in the air as gigantic waves lap onto the deck. He notices a young deckhand who is attempting to hold the sails steady. Panic grows on his face as they flap hard against his pull. Dragging his leg behind him, Peter rushes to help. The rope immediately cuts into his hand leaving deep red lacerations across his palms. The rains flood the deck as people run to safety, but there is nowhere to hide. Suddenly a creaking noise causes the pair to look up. A flash across the mast of the ship hits without warning. Lightning strikes the wet wood sending shock waves across the boat. Peter drops the rope in distress. There is a small moment of relief before a second creak sounds. Longer than the first, it creates a deafening silence. Everybody looks up as the mast cracks with a thud. Peter darts to the edge of the ship, holding tightly to the rail. He looks back at the deck-hand. Peter can see that he is screaming but the sound is blocked by the thrashing of the rain. His leg, mangled and bloodied, is trapped under the weight of the mast. Peter scrambles to push the weight off but before he can make it -

The rain has stopped. The silence is different now. Deeper somehow. More intense. Peter closes his eyes cocooned in the warm sensation. When he opens them, a fog surrounds him and it takes longer than it should for Peter to realise he is underwater. A wooden blockade obstructs his path, his fallen comrades raining down around him as they descend to the depths like buried treasure. He holds his breath, wondering if this will be his last. The Captain falls beside him, a dead weight, plunging slowly into the fathoms below as though he is moving through honey. Through squinted eyes Peter watches as the Captain is engulfed by the darkness beneath him. With his oxygen running out, instinct kicks in and Peter drives upwards, kicking as hard as he can, searching for a gap in the watery barricade. With only one good leg, the swim takes Peter far longer than expected and he can feel his eyes tempting to close, each blink lasting twice as long as it should.

Without warning the atmosphere changes. Peter can feel the wind in his hair, making the estuary waters feel icy against his skin. He flings his eyes open to reveal the carnage around him. There is nothing still standing that is recognisable. Peter scrambles to grab onto a barrel just out of his reach. The circular cask rotates under his fingers, inching away from him. Eventually, and just in time, Peter is able to latch onto it. Bobbing around in the estuary's freezing waters, Peter glances up to where the lightning had struck, and for a moment, he is convinced he can see a figure moving deep in the centre of the storm.

High on top of the hill, Sarah looks down at what she has done. A lump rises in her throat as she battles to suppress the sudden welling of emotions stirring within her. There are no signs of life below. Horrified, Sarah can no longer bear to look at the water. Instead, she begins to weep as she walks down the Broadway towards her empty house, the rain falling around her in sorrowful condolence.

THE TWITCH MARCH

DIANN WEBB

Taken from my allotment journal and extracts from my memoir, 'Simply Me'

Allotment 1990

On the face of it, it's just five rods of land, but it's something I have wanted for several years...an allotment of my own. £7.50 rent paid to the society and I am up and running. Clearly, I will have to buy some tools of my own, but now I am managing with dad's old fork and rake. An old shopping trolley is my only mode of transporting everything to and fro. Despite the February weather, I can't wait to get started.

Saturday:

Although its cold and wet it's easy to dig in places. The edges have a lot of twitch grass, (which they tell me is hard to get rid of,) and I am not sure what to do with the hill at the back of the plot by the rickety fence that hides a ditch. This area is a complete jungle of bindweed, nettles and bramble and I begin to feel guilty that I have intruded into the homes of the creatures underfoot.

This little piece of earth has become my saving grace. I am going through a bad patch, mostly worry about my elderly parents and the shenanigans that go on in their house at Avenue Rd Westcliff. Fortunately, I am living in England at the moment, so I am able to keep an eye on them. There seems to be no way out of the turmoil and worry that I am experiencing. But here, with a shovel in my hand, filthy dirty with a mind full of vegetables and snails there is no room for anything else, and so I can step outside myself allowing a different *me* to emerge.

I did five hours digging during the week. Mum came down on Friday and helped clear a bit of twitch. I have discovered that it needs to be cut back with shears before I can dig it up, and remove every bit of root, lest it re-grow. My friend Joy has given me some old carpet to smother some of it to prevent it getting worse.

Sunday:

Up early this morning to get to the allotment stores where I met some other diggers. Got lots of advice. Stocked up with potatoes, peas, and runner beans. I'm also planning to have a flower bed. On the list are gladioli, sweet peas, tagetes and snapdragons for starters.

It's so peaceful here, just a stone's throw from where I live, so handy, only a short walk away. There are two allotment sites in Manchester Drive, the West, and the East, which nestle in a 'dip' in the land. Prittle Brook is to the south of the site. Its flow depends entirely on the weather. I remember it overflowing in the 1960s after an enormous amount of rain, (my garden backs onto the brook). It made quite a din as it raged along. My anxiety increased on seeing a canoe pass by in the road! When the water was no more than a foot from my front door, I was on the verge of taking my newborn son, the dog, cat and all the kittens upstairs. Miraculously the rain stopped and began to recede. Mum was with me at the time and had to catch a bus home...so she simply took off her shoes, rolled up her trousers and waded across the road, up Grange Park Dr to the bus stop on the London Rd. *So far, no more flooding since!*

March:

Still digging. I have prepared the potato plot and it's now ready. Mum's helping to tidy up the raspberry canes. On removing an old plastic bag, I discovered loads of snails hibernating underneath, so I replaced it to catch some more. But now I'm worried what to do with them? *I re-located them by the brook on the way home.* But it's going to be an ongoing problem, maybe if I give them something to eat…a few cabbage leaves and tasty morsels, they would leave my seedlings alone!

Allotment 1998

My Allotment journal has been rather neglected lately due to other things.

My phone rang this morning at 6am as I was getting ready for work, it was Dad.

"You will have to come round; we've been burgled and Mother has disappeared." I called a taxi and sped off. I arrived to find Dad reading his newspaper and the place a mess, furniture tipped over, even the TV.

"What on earth has happened?" I ask. "I must have been hit over the head, I woke up on the floor and Mother has been kidnapped."

"Good grief."

Holding my breath, I look for Mum (who is never up at 6am). I call upstairs and make my way to her bedroom which was always locked (to keep Dad out). The door had been locked from the inside, so things look promising.

"Mum, Mum," I shout.

Mum is fairly deaf so it was pointless really. Ah! The sound of her snoring came through the door, thank the Lord. Eventually she hears me banging and opens the door to see what all the fuss is about. Dad must have been *thirsty* that night- too many barley wines and whisky- and fell about overturning furniture, blacked out, woke up, thought it was 6pm. Mum was not in her chair or in the kitchen so he had raised the alarm.

Thanks, Dad!

March:

I have a resident Robin who is hard to spot. He has a habit of suddenly appearing at my feet and if he is not careful, I fear he will be chopped in half with my spade A frog also had a lucky escape…he suffered quite a headache but survived!

Surprise! I have found some rhubarb which I had accidentally covered with soil, I had been walking all over it. Sowed an assortment of seeds. Leeks, carrots, peabeans and broad beans.

April:

Flower buds have appeared on the raspberries, but the blackcurrant and redcurrant bushes need a lot of attention as they are smothered in bindweed. Began to dig up the hill to level it. Found some strawberry plants and some more rhubarb amongst the weeds.

Summer:

Robin has disappeared. Dug up three slowworms, found a toad by the ditch and discovered some asparagus. The raspberries are prolific, managed to sell a few lbs. Still working on propagating the strawberries. Carrots were tasty, but small. Onions abundant, *not chewed upon by anything!* Blackfly spoiled the runners and the broad beans, so not a good crop, but all in all, a good first summer.

I am horrified to hear that the other 'plotters' have nicknamed me 'Lilo Lil', after one of the characters in a T.V series called 'Bread,' who used to give 'favours' to one of the main characters in his allotment shed. *I know I wear short shorts, and a skimpy halter top, but my back aches too much for favours!*

There is no finer place to be 'in the moment' then here. No matter about the raging backache, and the fingernails that now look like claws, it's my little piece of heaven and I am surrounded with like-minded people all cursing the slugs and snails, so I am not alone.

Stress free days don't last long. Today as I entered my parents' house, I found myself walking over a lot of crunchy stuff which completely covered the carpet, giving off noxious fumes. With a hankie over my nose, I crunch my way down the hall to the kitchen.

"Dad, what on earth is that stuff all over the carpet?"

"Slug pellets, we've got slugs."

"How many," I ask, expecting a plague of biblical proportions.

"Just one," he replies. "Can't stand them, horrid slimy things, have to get rid of it!"

Both Mum and Dad have become muddled. Mum freezes cabbages and lettuces and then complains they are inedible. Teaspoons have disappeared except for one. I found the rest in the sideboard drawer. She has also hidden the remote control down the side of her armchair so Dad can't fiddle with it. A lot of my time is taken up with looking for misplaced false teeth, walking sticks, spectacles, and Dad's favourite medal (a long service award from British Telecom which he sleeps with under his pillow).

August:

The man on the next plot seems to be an expert on most things, but today he is complaining. I'm afraid I showed off a bit and pointed to my beauties. (Tomatoes).

"Beginner's luck" was his quick reply.

Not having a shed, I have prepared a hiding place for my tools out of a few planks with a piece of plastic on top, covered with a few dead branches and weeds.

I must look a sight. Remember the T.V show, The Good Life? (I'm the one in the wellies wearing a sweater with different coloured sleeves with straw in her hair). If my friend Pat were here to help me, she would no doubt present herself as 'Margot,' completely co-ordinated with immaculate hair, manicured nails, and a posh pair of wellies!

Heading for home. Backache, nettle stung, weary, dirty, with broken nails. Hungry. Arrived home…flung all the filthy produce out the back. Took some painkillers and lay on the floor, after which I had beans on toast…*not a greenfly in sight.*

I'm so pleased with the way my woven bower of honeysuckle and jasmine at the back have intertwined. The heady perfume has mingled with the orange blossom which began as a cutting from mum. It's an absolute delight and a row of sweet peas hides me from the other plotters if I need shade or solitude. Sometimes I just need to clear my mind of problems.

After much digging and levelling, the hill has now gone, and I miss it but now at last I can get to the red currants and a very neglected blackcurrant bush. Strawberries are abundant, made jam, froze some, sold some. Made green tomato chutney with those that didn't ripen. One beef tomato weighed 1lb 5oz! Home grown produce taste so much better than shop bought especially the tomatoes and strawberries.

Sitting amongst the vegetables and flowers stimulated childhood memories. Uncle Barney used to take me to his allotment and I was quite happy to sit amongst the cabbages, *this is where babies came from…so they said.* My scream brought uncles to my side and they quickly removed a huge slimy snail from my leg and Uncle Alfie was extremely upset when cousin B and I picked the flowers off his tomato plants!

My plot has really blossomed this summer, it fizzed with bees and was a blaze of flowers and produce, I even had luck with butternut squash and a pumpkin. Courgettes and leeks were good too, but the day I decided to harvest the sweetcorn some animal got there first! The rosemary has grown into a large bush, it has such a strong pungent aroma I can't resist touching it, and the marjoram is smothered in bees, as is the lavender, which will make nice lavender bags later, maybe on rainy days.

September:

Mum phoned this morning and said Dad's not well so I called in to see what the problem was. I arrived to find Dad has a tummy ache and diarrhoea (I know Dad likes mouldy cheese; furry beyond belief)! but I ask him anyway…

"What have you been eating?"

"Crabs."

"And where did you keep them?"

"In the bathroom cabinet."

"Why?"

"To warm them up a bit."

"For how long?"

"Two or three days."

Well, that solved that then.

October:

The twitch marched on always needing constant attention. A mouse has made a nest in my old spade handle that is hidden under the plastic at the back. *One reason not to dig.* Saw three Kestrels fighting in the sky, found a dead fox by the compost heap and noticed a voyeur crouching in the ditch, very creepy. I stared at him and he disappeared, and thank goodness someone has kindly disposed of the decomposing fox for me.

I was very surprised one afternoon to hear quite a commotion in the Oak tree. I am familiar with our local bird song but this was sharp and grating. Aha, it's a green parrot!

More trouble at home! Along with the usual shopping requests of oxtail and

ducks eggs I now have an extra something to get Dad.

The Flea Collar

"I want you to get me a flea collar," said Dad.

"But you haven't got a cat."

"I know."

"So why do you need a flea collar?"

"It's for me."

"It won't fit round your neck."

"I'll wear it on my wrist."

"But WHY do you want one?"

"I itch." *(Dad didn't have fleas; the itch was caused by liver damage).*

I tire easily these days, so one sunny afternoon I lay down on an untidy patch of grass for a rest. A rustling sound made me turn my head, I expected to see a mouse, but 'no'...it's a snake slithering by.

Lying here on the twitch admiring my stately gladioli, I can let go of the worries for a while. Watching Nature... nothing wasted...everything is recycled, the falling leaves enrich the soil for the coming year, even the snails fertilise the soil as they munch their way along!

I have learned such a lot from the other 'plotters' and mother always gives me advice about seed sowing times which is very helpful, but nowadays, because my time is limited, I have filled up any gaps with flowers as I haven't time to tend vegetables.

'The seasons come...and the seasons go.' Each season teaching me something different. The excitement of spring... the abundance of summer...the blaze of autumn and finally the cold sleep of winter.

Allotment 1999

The allotment is on the back burner and the journal is empty of entries due to the upheaval at home. I have had to give up work almost entirely, I can only manage to get in a couple of days a week.

The phone rang this morning it was doctor, with the results of my X-ray. The diagnosis is spinal arthritis. Doc says it won't get better, it's degenerative, but to stay active.

February 7th

Dad died, so now living with mum as she has dementia and cannot cope alone. Everything is extremely difficult; I am tired beyond belief.

Allotment 2000

August:

Mum died, followed by my sister four months later. It helps to be on the allotment where I can sort out my thoughts and feelings, and the practicalities of sorting things out after a death can be overwhelming. It seems as if 'probate' has taken over my life...*will it ever end?*

Amongst the weeds I have managed to locate the beetroot

which I'm so pleased with. They would have been larger if it had rained more. Because walking to the water butt and carrying watering cans back to the plot is terribly tiring, I'm afraid the produce has had to 'make do.'

Feathers and Angels

One afternoon thoughts of my mother lingered, she loved helping me by picking her favourite vegetables, runner beans. It was a hot afternoon so I sat down to have a rest and a cuppa, when I noticed a tiny feather high in the sky, wafting about on the breeze. I watched it, willing it to land at my feet, but it blew away out of sight, so I got on with some more digging, till another rest was required, and there to my amazement, upon the chair lay a tiny feather!

Angels and feathers: It is said that a guardian angel is sending a message of love, comfort, hope, and peace. Hello mum!

Whilst living with mum, my plot suffered a lot of neglect. Sid, a few plots over, has kindly been keeping it tidy for me. However, I finally found the time to take up the spade again, and despite the arthritic pain carried on. Sid seems to have disappeared for good so I assumed he had passed away as he was quite elderly. Then I did something awful. I helped myself to a root of his Red-Hot Poker plant. *In memory!* Time passed. Sid eventually re-appeared looking fit and well and… *furious.*

"Some bugger has pinched some of my Red-Hot Pokers. You can't trust anybody!" *I crept silently away with tail between legs!*

Allotment 2001

Dean Boshell was found dead on one of the plots, they say it was an execution by shooting. There were allegations of organised crime and bribery. It's all very worrying.

I was discussing our safety with a lady two plots over and she described one day, hearing a loud sound and felt a pain in her thigh but didn't make any connection between the two. It was only when visiting the doctor with an unrelated issue that he commented on the large bruise on her thigh, saying it looked like a shot from a B.B gun, (a rifle!) My worrying find was a bolt from a crossbow near my runner beans!

Autumn:

One sunny afternoon, all was quiet till cracking, popping sounds came from the boundary fence, where a few unused plots were covered with very dry grass. When puffs of smoke appeared, I realised someone had thrown some fireworks over the fence. It didn't take a few seconds for a flash fire to speed along the plots at an alarming rate. I called 999 and opened the main gate before I left for home.

December:

It was just before Christmas and I nipped down to the allotment to pick some Brussel sprouts. I arrived at my plot and scanned the area but there wasn't a sprout in sight! All that remained was a row of stalks...not a leaf or anything edible left. I might add the pigeons had left a grand amount of droppings, so it was well fertilised for the following year.

***

Years have now passed and I am weary, my plot is weary, the soil is depleted. Someone has kindly offered to share a pile of manure with me, which really 'pongs' but I haven't got the strength to carry bucketful's of it to my plot. I was lucky enough to find some keen people to work half the plot with me but now I am afraid it is with a certain amount of sadness that I have to say goodbye to my 'green haven,' *and the relentless march of the twitch.* My plot has not only fed me in body and spirit but added to my knowledge of growing one's own food, even if half of it was eaten by other hungry critters.

I am now looking at my little garden with 'different eyes.' Tomato plants can go there, onions will be fine, maybe some beet and radishes, and of course, not forgetting the runner beans...just for mum...*maybe she will reward me with another feather.*

JUDGEMENT DAY

RICHARD KURTI

Was that a Swastika, or was she imagining it?

Miss Godwin peered at the half-finished painting, trying to make sense of the pencil lines that would soon be covered by patches of colour as the picture progressed.

When Southend Council first announced its *Celebrate the City* art competition, Miss Godwin had immediately thought of Callum, the most talented sixth-form student she'd taught in her twenty years at Southend Grammar School.

"I dunno, miss," he'd replied, eyes glancing at everything in the art room but his teacher. "Competitions are for kids. Like getting a Blue Peter badge."

"But think how impressive this would look on your UCAS application."

"Really?"

"For sure. Places at the top art schools are like hen's teeth. You need to play every card you can get your hands on."

Callum's heavy brow furrowed. "But I've got my portfolio."

"They'll all have dazzling portfolios. But the painting that wins *Celebrate the City* will be hung in Southend's Council Chamber. Just think how impressive *that* would be on your CV."

"I suppose."

Miss Godwin knew that Callum had set his sights on going to the Slade School of Fine Art in London, and although she had every faith in his talent, Slade had a formidable reputation and attracted applicants from all over the world. Miss Godwin should know because she was a Slade alumna and loved basking in the achievements of her cohort. Some had become famous, some notorious, one had even won the Turner Prize, and Miss Godwin never missed an opportunity to drop the odd name or two. "I remember when I had to lend him my brushes because he'd turned up to a life class stoned out of his mind," she would smile as she stood in front of some impressive canvas in the Tate Modern.

For herself, Miss Godwin had navigated a different path, nurturing the talents of the next generation; but if Callum could win *Celebrate the City* and also gain a place at Slade, it would prove that in her own quiet way she had been keeping the embers of fine art glowing in the wilderness.

She slid her reading glasses down from her neatly bobbed hair.

Callum's painting was certainly very accomplished. Inspired by 1930s railway posters that promised 'Happy Holidays by the Sea!', it was a panorama of the esplanade, populated with clean-cut families having wholesome fun. But in Callum's hands, the idea had become a clever interplay between past and present. The modern university building, the Forum, and some sparkling executive apartments had been blended into the vision of the past, creating an image that was both contemporary yet tapped into the undercurrent of nostalgia that ran through Southend. It captured the chip on the city's shoulder – that nagging sense of grievance that the golden age had passed.

Crucially, the picture was accessible, and that, Miss Godwin felt, was a sign of Callum's artistic maturity. While other students were venting their teenage angst, Callum had understood that great art didn't rant, it whispered.

All that would be undermined, however, if he was going to twist Southend's Pier into the shape of a Swastika.

Miss Godwin picked up a magnifying glass and studied the pencil marks on the canvas. One line jutted out from the beach and stretched across the water, but where the pier-head should have been, Callum had drawn the walkways as a set of crossed lines. The shape was right-facing and tilted at an angle, so it wasn't the ancient Sanskrit symbol. No, Hitler had created this version of the Swastika to glorify the Nazis.

Why would Callum scar a beautiful image with such clumsy symbolism?

Two days later, Callum was working on the painting in class. Affecting an air of nonchalance, Miss Godwin sidled behind him; to her dismay, she saw that he had now painted the pencil lines in black acrylic, making the Swastika-pier permanent.

"So ... what do you think this picture is saying?" Miss Godwin ventured.

Callum shrugged. "Just playing with ideas."

"And the pier? Is that a Cubist approach?"

"I don't really know."

"It's certainly ... bold," Miss Godwin tiptoed. "I wonder what it means?"

"You always told us art speaks for itself."

"I did, yes. But..."

Callum stopped painting and looked at his teacher. "Have I done something wrong, miss?"

"Only you can make the creative choices. But today's world is so divided, I wonder if your imagery might ... alienate people?"

Callum dabbed his brush into a swirl of pearl blue and started touching it onto the waves.

"If you want to be successful, Callum, you need people's support. Not their hostility."

"Maybe what people see in a picture says more about them, miss?"

"Maybe."

Nothing else was said, but the exchange must have irked Callum, because at the end of the lesson he wrapped his canvas in a large cloth and put it under his arm. "I'm going to work on it over the weekend, miss."

"Okay. Fine."

Miss Godwin decided to push all thoughts of Callum from her mind. In any case, she had plenty to occupy her, as she was busy packaging up her own painting for entry into the prestigious Royal Academy's Summer Exhibition in London. Of her thirty-four attempts, this was the first time Miss Godwin had made it past the photographic submission stage and been asked to send in the work itself.

Every year she had meticulously studied the comments made by the judges in their rejection letters, trying to extract every last drop of wisdom. And every year she had used that feedback to inform a new painting that might finally delight the selection committee. This time, she was convinced she had cracked it; friends who had seen *Mods and Rockers* loved it, and the painting had fifty-seven likes on her Instagram feed, which made it her top-ranking post.

As she swathed the painting in bubble wrap, Miss Godwin felt grateful that she had complete control over her time. Fellow teachers were torn in so many directions, constantly trying to juggle work and family, but Miss Godwin had turned her home into a personal sanctuary: both spare bedrooms were permanent studios, and the dining room doubled as a store for her finished pictures.

As she passed the package over the counter in the DHL office, Miss Godwin's imagination ran wild. What a summer this would be: her own painting hanging in the Royal Academy, Callum's displayed in the Council Chamber, followed by him winning a place at Slade ... Miss Godwin would be Artist, Teacher, and Mentor. No one would be able to ignore her any longer.

"What's the value of the item?" the clerk asked in a flat voice.

"I'm sorry?"

"The value. For insurance. What should I put?"

"Oh ... it's hard to say."

"Up to £250. Up to £5000 or £10,000 and above?"

"Er, what's the difference in price?"

Mr Bower checked his watch. "I only have a few minutes. Governors' meeting at six."

"Of course," Miss Godwin ushered him to the easels.

It was unusual for the Head teacher to take this kind of interest in classroom work, for his was a world of budgets and Ofsted, but it was a mark of the prestige of the competition that he had asked to see all three entries the school was making. Secretly, Miss Godwin thought it would be the perfect opportunity to steer Callum's painting back onto the right course, but he hadn't turned up, so she would have to settle for showing Daisy and Hannah's paintings instead.

Proud Essex Girls captured a lairy nightclub moment in bubble gum colours, and although it was striking, this was not the image the city wanted to project. *Howzat!* was closer to the mark, a watercolour depicting the annual Boys v Teachers cricket match. Southend was inordinately proud of its grammar school, so this picture would resonate even though the composition was rather bland.

"Very nice," Mr Bower said. "But wasn't there a third entry?"

"Oh, Callum emailed to say he wasn't feeling very well," Miss Godwin fibbed. "But his painting is finished."

"Something inspiring, I hope?"

"A beautiful sunny day on the esplanade."

"Excellent. A positive image for the city. Just what the Mayor's looking for. No more of this 'talking the place down' nonsense." Mr Bower checked his watch again. "Unfortunately, I won't be able to come along to the event itself. Been invited to address the National Conference of Head teachers." He beamed a smile at the sixth formers. "But I wish you the very best of luck."

The following Wednesday morning, twenty-three students from schools across the borough, paintings clutched under their arms, entered the council chamber to find it buzzing. Proud teachers were taking their places in the tiered seating, while students were directed towards a circle of easels to set up for the judging. A photographer flitted around the chamber, capturing the event from all angles.

Callum deliberately chose an easel at the back of the circle; timing was important, and he didn't want anyone raising the alarm too soon.

The Town Clerk banged a gavel and called for silence as Mayor Duckfield strode into the chamber, chain of office riding high on his portly chest. He went to the podium and waxed lyrical about civic pride and local talent, but Callum wasn't really listening because he felt suddenly queasy; sweat broke on his forehead as if he were about to vomit. Maybe this was a bad idea. Maybe he should just bolt for the fire doors and disappear. He glanced around the chamber, trying to work out the best escape route-

Too late. The Mayor had stopped talking and turned his attention to the paintings.

Callum watched anxiously as he made his way from easel to easel, nodding, scrutinizing, exchanging a few words with the students as if he were royalty. Finally, he arrived at Callum's painting...

And froze.

He blinked twice. "What is the meaning of this?"

The quiet venom in the Mayor's voice was terrifying. Callum wanted to answer, he *needed* to answer, the truth had to come out, but his tongue was glued to the inside of his mouth.

"I think you should explain yourself," Duckfield said.

Callum glanced at the audience, searching for Miss Godwin, desperate for her to rush to his rescue. But when he saw her, she looked down to avoid his gaze.

"Nothing to say?" the Mayor goaded.

"Art speaks for itself," Callum managed to croak.

"Is that so?" Mayor Duckfield picked up Callum's painting. "Thousands of people from this city fought against the Nazis. Many never came home. They paid the ultimate price. And this student," he held the picture up to show the audience, "thinks it's clever to mock their sacrifice."

Callum felt the ripple of indignation as people realized that their beloved pier, the pride of the city, had been painted in the shape of a huge Swastika.

"Shame on you," someone in the audience heckled.

"Indeed." The Mayor glared at Callum. "I think you owe us all an apology."

"It's you who needs to apologize." The words escaped from Callum's mouth before he could stop them.

"What did you say?" Duckfield gasped.

"On behalf of those chains of office," Callum pointed to the Mayor's chest.

"Disqualify him!" the heckler urged.

"No, no." The Mayor was playing to the crowd. "This I want to hear. What exactly do I have to apologize for?"

It was now or never. Callum had to find his voice, or all his hard work would have been for nothing.

"In 1935, the Mayor of Southend led an official visit to Frankfurt to kiss the Nazi ring."

"What on earth are you talking about?"

Callum cleared his throat and took a deep breath. "Burgermeister Linder greeted the Southend delegation in full Nazi uniform. Your predecessor gave a hearty toast to the Fuhrer. They stood shoulder to shoulder and made the Hitler salute. They celebrated being from one Anglo-Saxon race, with shared blood in their veins." Callum ignored the cold sweat trickling down his back and looked into Duckfield's blue eyes. "I think Southend's Mayor loved Hitler, and this painting exposes that ugly truth."

"Nonsense!" The Mayor's jowls quivered. "You're making this up!"

Callum rummaged in his pocket, "Here's a copy of the article. From the archives of the Southend Standard."

The Mayor snatched the paper from Callum's hand and screwed it into a ball. "What you fail to appreciate, is that many important people went on diplomatic missions to Germany in the 1930s. The Duke of Windsor for one. Because no one knew what was coming."

"That's a lie."

"How dare you?"

"They all knew. This was after the Nuremberg rallies. After the torchlight parades. After Frankfurt had sacked all the Jews who worked for the city."

"Who are you to judge?" The Mayor looked down his nose at Callum. "You're not a historian. You're just a child."

Callum opened his hand to reveal a small gold coin. "This was sewn into my grandfather's coat when he was my age, when he escaped from Vienna. He kissed goodbye to his parents at Westbahnhof station and never saw them again. Three years later, they were deported to Belarus and murdered by the Nazis. My grandfather taught me that if you don't call out Fascism when you see it, it always ends in murder and misery."

A strange look crept across Mayor Duckfield's face. "Why does everything always have to be about the Jews?" He thrust the painting back at Callum. "You need to get a life, young man. And you can start by getting out of this council chamber." The Mayor nodded to the Town Clerk, and moments later a security guard was striding towards the stage.

Callum focused on the sound of the clock in the Head teacher's study. *Tick-tick-tick-tick-tick.* He could tell from the agitated movement of Mr Bower's hands that he was in trouble, but he only heard every other word.

"Ingratitude ... humiliation ... apology ... immature..."

Callum endured the onslaught stoically. When it was over, he left the office and sloped home alone.

Miss Godwin had hoped to keep a low profile until things calmed down, but when Callum still hadn't returned to school after three days, she decided to phone him.

"Callum, I know you're upset, but I'm sure there's a way through this."

"Every word was the truth, miss."

"It's water under the bridge now."

"Not to me."

"What matters is putting this behind you and focusing on the future. I know Mr Bower said he wouldn't support your university application, but I'm prepared to coach you in my own time. We can't let a moment of madness affect your whole life."

"Thank you, miss, but no."

"Come on, Callum. Don't give up. Show some backbone."

"I'm not giving up. You see, it found its way onto TikTok."

"What did?"

"Everything. What I said. The picture. The Mayor. It went viral as #Swastika-On-Sea. Look..."

Miss Godwin's phone pinged. She opened the alert and

saw a video snippet of Callum being escorted from the council chamber. It had 1.2 million likes.

"Slade saw it and reached out to me," Callum said.

"What? How?"

"I don't know, but they've offered me a place."

"The Slade School of Art approached you?" Miss Godwin was stunned. "And offered you a place?"

"Yes."

"That's ... that's ..." Miss Godwin felt as if she was drowning. "Well ... congratulations."

"Thank you, miss."

"Yes ... well done."

It was a relief to hang up the phone. She was pleased for Callum, of course she was. But it wasn't just that. It was more complicated. 1.2 million views. How did that happen?

Miss Godwin was still trying to untangle her emotions as she prepared dinner ... and then the doorbell chimed. She hurried down the hallway and opened the front door to reveal a DHL courier clutching a parcel.

"Sign here."

Miss Godwin's heart skipped a beat, she knew exactly what this was - her own painting, returned from the Royal Academy. She tore open the packaging searching for the judges' comments, but this time there wasn't even a letter.

Her fists clenched. She had played the game so perfectly, researched this year's judges and tested her picture out on friends. Everyone liked it. And now she was rejected. Again.

Miss Godwin, Artist, Teacher and Mentor, slumped onto the sofa and wept.

When her tears subsided, she looked again at the picture. It depicted a Mod and a Rocker, trousers rolled up, paddling next to each other in the sea. It was supposed to be a social comment presented in a witty way, but for the first time, Miss Godwin saw the painting for what it really was – a stupid piece of nostalgia. The sort of thing you'd see on a birthday card. A picture designed to please an ageing aunt.

She remembered her first week at Slade, feeling that she was part of a generation that would change everything. But that young Rebecca Godwin would have been ashamed of this middle-of-the-road piece of trash. She would have been ashamed of this neat house with its matching furniture and the polished car on the drive.

Miss Godwin stood up and gazed into the mirror. She had sacrificed so much, and all she had to show for it was a pile of rejection letters.

Mr Bower looked at her in disbelief. "Resigning?"

"Yes."

"Please, Miss Godwin, don't let this unfortunate incident with the Mayor tarnish your years of-"

"It's not that. It's about me."

"But that's the point. I was going to offer you an exhibition space here at the school, in the entrance hall."

"I'm sorry?"

"For your own art. Where all the visitors and parents can see it. As a thank you for everything you've done. Please, stay with us."

Miss Godwin hesitated ... then shook her head. "People come to school to learn. And finally, I have. From the very student I was teaching."

As she walked out of the school gates for the last time, Miss Godwin felt young again, even though she had greying hair and a body plagued with aches. She walked and walked, along the seafront and up the cliffs, until she was gazing out over the pier.

Miss Godwin drew a deep breath and smiled.

The artist who had been buried inside her for so long was stirring once more, and this time she would connect. *Really* connect. To hell with what other people thought.

She was Miss Godwin no longer; now she was Rebecca.

Footnote: A detailed report of Mayor A.T. Edwards' visit to the Nazi administration in Frankfurt can be found in The Southend Standard, October 10th, 1935. It is available on microfilm from Southend Central Library at The Forum.

NEVER NEVER LAND

CATHERINE THORNTON

Beyond the pier and the shimmering sands,
Lies a realm that can defies life's demands,
A world of enchantment, where time stands still,
Where wishes and fantasies are fulfilled.

The carousel spins with music and grace,
Painting smiles on each of their face,
Children's laughter fills the air,
In this magical place, they need not to care.

Pirates would roam, and fairies would dance,
In this Never Never Land – a second chance,
To be a child, to let worries go,
And let your imagination freely flow.

Mermaids sing by the water's edge,
While lost boys hide in the reeds and sedge,
Peter Pan leads with a mischievous grin,
Adventures to make your head spin

. . .

So come, my dear , and take grandma's hand,
To this wondrous place in Southend sand,
Where childhood dreams forever expand,
In our very own Never Never Land.

GROWING UP IN LEIGH-ON-SEA

JIM RICHES

A *Boy's Journey of Wonder and Imagination*

In 2018 I moved back to Leigh on Sea after living in Kent for several years. I missed my home town, I missed the sea and the walks I had done so many times in the past. I wanted to get back to my favourite places such as Belfairs Woods and Hadleigh Castle to see if they both still held the same attraction for me after so many years away. I was soon rediscovering the town and countryside where I had grown up. Retracing the steps I had taken in my youth reminded me why I felt that I belonged in this area.

My formative years were spent at Fairways Schools in The Fairway, which is very close to Belfairs Woods. Virtually every spare moment outside of school I walked and played in the Woods. I was always an active kid, sandwiched as I was between an elder and younger sister, I had to find my own hobbies as dolls and the Bay City Rollers didn't hold my interest.

I was lucky enough to make many friends at school, and we often played together in the early evenings and at week-ends. I was equally happy being on my own. Apart from being active and being able to walk for miles each day without seeming to tire, I also had an inquisitive mind and wanted to know as much as I could about my home area. Belfairs in particular seemed massive to me as a child, but old maps show that it was once part of Epping Forest: so what remains today is 1200 acres or so of a once huge, forested area of south Essex. I was intrigued and enchanted by it almost as soon as I could walk. The park has thickly wooded areas where it is easy to lose yourself in deep thought and maybe even work out a troubled mind. The early evening birdsong in Springtime seems to indicate the woods are coming alive again. At dusk, foxes and badgers forage, and the occasional woodpecker is heard but rarely seen. Children play among the trees, dogs run freely with no danger from traffic, and countless squirrels run from both dogs and humans. Woven in amongst the trees is a golf course, and there is also a horse trotting track around the boundary of the woods.

In my very early years, walking through the woods was restricted to being with Mum and Dad, along with the two girls and our faithful collie. This helped me to develop a mental map of the park, and all the roads and paths which led in or out of the woods. A section containing the most ancient woodland was declared a nature reserve in 1938, with some trees said to be 1,000 years old. The reserve is thickly forested and bordered to the south and west by the towns and villages of Hadleigh and Daws Heath. It therefore allowed plenty of scope for exploring further afield.

I was about ten when I also took a huge interest in the ruins of Hadleigh Castle. This came to be after one family walk through the woods and nature reserve where we made our way through the streets of Hadleigh to the country park in which the Castle ruins and grounds are sited, on the north bank of the Thames. The ruins fascinated me. I often wondered, and to this day still do, what it must have been like when it was complete and occupied. All that remains is one almost complete round tower, less than half of another, and some low walls. Several other chunks of rock and stone are scattered around the hilltop site, some of which have fallen from where they once stood due to many landslips that have occurred almost since it was first built. I must have driven my schoolteachers mad with my constant questions, and the librarian at Leigh Library too with my regular requests of her for local history books.

At that age, and of course, being years before the internet could provide so many answers, my imagination had to suffice: Not that was a bad thing then, I would often try to put myself back some 500 years and wander up to the castle in my daydreams. Belfairs Park and Hadleigh Castle became a growing presence in my life.

Belfairs also contains another source of entertainment for some, for weaving its way through the trees is a popular public 18-hole golf course. My dad was a keen golfer, and we spent hours walking around the course, or more precisely in the trees looking for lost balls. I wasn't that bothered by golf back then, but it was always nice to find a new ball and exchange it for a shilling with my dad. We had to earn our pocket money and that was very easy money for me, I soon learned where most balls would disappear from the tee of every hole.

Time didn't stand still, my days at Fairways seemed to pass by quickly and before I knew much about handicaps and eagles, I was heading off to Westcliff High School.

I wasn't the best pupil that ever walked through the gates of Westcliff High, I did okay but I was so easily sidetracked and I preferred my evening walks to sitting indoors working out how A could equal B if you divided it by 3.14 and a pie of some sort. I knew then that I'd never need that answer in adult life, but I did want to know more about local history. It comes as no surprise then that my best subjects were history and geography. Much as I got on with many of the teachers, I clashed with my history teacher. History was renamed Classics for a year or two, and my teacher didn't like me. It wasn't unfair, I couldn't stand him either. I asked him once if we could explore the history of Hadleigh Castle, and what a mistake that simple question turned out to be. He told me in no uncertain terms that it was not going to happen in his class, and we would study Greek mythology. However, he couldn't deter me from my own out of school activities and almost obsessive time spent in Belfairs Park and over at the Castle.

When I walk in Belfairs now, my mind often wanders back to those days when my dad was there with me, and I wonder what he would make of the changes that have been made there in more recent years, with a lot more forestry maintenance having taken place to thin out some of the thicker wooded areas we used to lose ourselves in. He worked nights so it was always a real treat to be able to spend time with him on the occasional evening that he didn't go to work. We had a favourite tree that we'd climb, we named it The Seat due to the number of low branches that grew out from the trunk at right angles. We sat on them and watched the golfers hit their shots from the 16th tee, with the tree being 75 yards or so on the left from the tee. We also named that entire section Bomb Alley as hooked shots would often fly into the woods near The Seat. That tree is still there today, and I think of the happy time playing there with my sisters and my dad each time I walk past it. Dad was just becoming a friend as well as a father to me when fate struck its cruel blow and ripped our family apart. He was in Southend Hospital after a heart attack, but was told he needed to go to a London hospital for surgery. I wished him well on the morning that he was taken to Bethnal Green chest clinic, as I trudged off to school. My words to him are still so vivid: "See you in a couple of weeks". He gave his customary flashing smile but didn't say much more than "Yeah, hope so". It was the last time we spoke. He died a couple of weeks later, not having recovered from the bypass surgery which today is routine. That was it, my Dad was gone forever and he left me alone in a house full of females. My sisters and I have always been close, and maybe that period of our lives set that mutual fondness in stone. We all have different lives now, but no one will ever come between us. Well, maybe the Bay City Rollers did for a while.

It was just after Dad died that I started to walk more and more alone in Belfairs. I ventured further out. Wherever there was a path, I wanted to know where it went. Maybe it was a reaction to losing Dad in that I needed to refocus and take an interest in something else, but without a doubt, those paths which sometimes ended up getting me lost, helped me find a new direction and ease the pain of loss. Walking through the woods now I can still recognise some of the other ancient trees, but they have also continued to grow and branch out.

Curiously, and again not long after my dad passed, one of my school pals asked me if I'd like to play golf. Though I enjoyed my own company, often there was a knock on our door and one of my friends suggested a walk, a game of golf, football, or anything that involved getting me out and about.

At least I'd have a fair idea of where my wayward shots might be among the trees, as I knew the woods so well. I began the evening walks looking for lost balls again. Dad was still with me of course, his voice in my mind reminding me where the best places to look were. He was never wrong.

The woods don't just hold sad memories for me, far from it. We were on a school cross-country run, starting at Westcliff's playing fields and along the then dual carriageway to Belfairs Park. The route took us through the woods as far as a white gate that leads out to Daws Heath and eventually Hadleigh, but we turned back at the gate to run along the horse trotting track and then beside Prittle Brook to emerge on Eastwood Road and a path which meanders back to the school.

Despite being fit, I wasn't a great long-distance runner. Short bursts were more for me. A small group of us were near the back of the group, and keeping an eye on the rear was a teacher new to the area. We learned years later that for various reasons he wasn't a good fit and only lasted a year or so before being moved on. We decided to play a trick on him, and what happened next just fell into our laps. The Southend United footballers were training in the woods and as we approached them, our plan came together in an instant. The plan was that we'd all disappear into the woods so that the teacher would lose sight of us. We spoke with a couple of the players and asked them to look out for a bearded man in a blue tracksuit who wasn't far behind us. We asked them to direct him through the white gate and to keep going, saying they had seen us go through there. Hours later, when we were back in school and having a lesson in the old science block that used to face Kenilworth Gardens, a taxi pulled up at the school gates. Out came our new teacher. He'd been to Hadleigh, bypassed the castle, ran across the downs, and along to Leigh Station at which point he gave up and called a cab. He must have run about 8 miles to our 3 or 4.

I was a member of the 11th Leigh Scout group, which was based at St Aidan's church hall in The Fairway. I was not a religious person, but as the group used the church's facilities, there was a clear path to church for those who wanted it. What I liked, was that the vicar didn't force religion on anyone at all. He also became a very good friend of mine.

The vicar, Don, and I had many great conversations. We understood each other and I was amazed when he respected my reasons for turning my back on religion. I just couldn't accept why my family had been torn apart by death. Then one of the people who did more than many to help me through it had also died. What was the point of praying to this guy who was there to care for all of us? With that attitude, you can imagine that Don and I could talk for days on end, as we often did. Tragically Don also passed away at a relatively early age, which for me reinforced the point I'd made to him.

In my later teens, I returned with a few others to help run the scout group. This was a particularly happy time of my life, coming so soon after the worst of times, and I believe that contrast of emotions finally toughened me up.

My school days came to an end at the age of 16. We needed money in the house, so further education was out of the question. Mum didn't work, she gave her time to bringing up three teenagers. So off I went into the big wide world. That was when I started to grow up at a much faster rate. I had to focus on a job, people relied on me and I relied on them. School hadn't taught me that, they seemed to shut the door behind me without offering me much clue as to what to expect next.

The headmaster was put out by my decision to leave at 16 and brushed me aside. I did have one very good ally there though, my maths and cricket master who became a good friend and a huge support as I tried to come to terms with being a breadwinner while barely out of short trousers. He had known my dad vaguely as they both enjoyed the 19th hole at Belfairs, the Woodcutters Arms. He was a good man and, in some ways, I suppose he, by fault or by design, took on some of the roles that would have been my dad's. We sometimes met for a drink and a chat. He was very supportive while I was finding my way with my first job. It was such a massive blow when he too passed away suddenly. I felt alone. I found it difficult to get too close to people for a while in case I lost them as well.

There was no escaping from my favourite places though, Belfairs Woods and Hadleigh Castle. The scout group only strengthened the bond I felt with those two places. We would do night hikes from one to the other, we would play 'British Bulldog' from one side of the castle ruins to the other. That could get quite feisty and many a scout would go home with bruises for trophies.

I studied the history of Hadleigh Castle. The one thing I had never known was that despite being built in the 13th century, it has since that time nearly always been little more than ruins. It was built when Henry III was king, by Hubert de Burgh who was a prominent castle builder at the time across England and Wales. Henry and Hubert fell out, and the castle was neglected until it was given to Queen Margaret and Edward I. He used it a couple of times as a base for hunting 'to the north of the castle', which would have been Belfairs Woods which then extended as far as what is now Hadleigh Country Park. Despite Edward III extending the castle in the mid-1300s, a flaw in de Burgh's plan became evident. The castle was built on a ridge of soft London clay. A series of landslips over the years left it in ruins, and much was sold off in the 1500s for its valuable stone.

There also remains doubt as to why the castle was even built: was it to protect London from the French invasions of the time, or was it just a convenient royal hunting retreat close to the capital? That has never been answered.

One of its last two remaining towers collapsed before I was born, but I do remember another landslip in the early 1970s. Thankfully since then, far more care has been taken of it, with English Heritage owning and supporting it. Even now when I walk to it from Leigh, the point where the remaining tower comes into view is a sight that inspires so much thought, so much imagination. It can be seen from quite a distance and despite its ruinous state, has always appeared quite imposing and acts as a comparison between the old and new when looking in the opposite direction to the bars, restaurants, cafes, and boutique shops in Leigh on Sea. My dogs used to love running up and down the hills surrounding it, though they were more interested in chasing rabbits than wondering who used to live there.

One summer's day my border collie, Mac, was walking along the edge of the grass away from the remaining tower. There had been yet another recent landslip and a flimsy orange plastic fence had been placed along the edge to warn people away from quite a perilous drop. A young family was having a picnic close by, but one of their children, maybe between 2 and 3 years old, had started to get very close to the plastic fence without anyone noticing. I then became aware that Mac had calmly stepped forward and placed himself between the fence and the child and nudged her back away from the edge. Her father then realised where she was and quickly retrieved her. Border collies of course have that natural herding instinct, but for one to realise the danger that a child was in and to then resolve the situation with no human command or intervention was mind-boggling. Some of Mac's ashes ended up in the same spot many years later, which gives me another reason to continue to pay my respects to the history of the place, ancient and modern.

The view from the ruins is vast, and on a clear day, you can see the tall buildings of London in the far distance to the west, and the wind farm way out in the Thames Estuary to the east. Kent opposite adds the backdrop with Canvey and Two Tree Island in the foreground. With a slight breeze, you can taste the salty sea air. It's a beautiful place to be and one I have enjoyed all my life.

SPANISH ESTATE

CAROLIN VOIGT

He could feel his heart beating. In front of him, the woman was lying on the road in the lights of his Range Rover. Her long dark hair had slipped out of a loose knot. Tight dress, high heels and a short white jacket. She looked like she was on her way to go out, maybe the pub nearby. When he saw her crossing the road, he had pressed down on the brakes, or was it the gas? That feeling of wanting to hit something came back.

It was a warm evening. The road was quiet, and nobody else was out, only the noise from the busy road behind him. Tidy gardens in front of well maintained and extended detached houses. Well fed children were in bed by now, as their parents enjoyed a glass of wine in front of the television. He had come off busy London Road to take this shortcut. As usual there was a traffic jam at those lights turning onto Highlands and he couldn't face to wait in a queue.

The day had started off badly. Linda had called and wanted to collect some of her stuff. He didn't want to see her, but she came to collect her favorite vase, putting it into her red handbag he had given her for their anniversary last year. 'Hopefully, that's it.' he grunted before slamming the door in her face.

In the afternoon, he met up with Pete. It was one of the new restaurants which opened in Leigh after the pandemic. Italian with a dark, tasteful interior. He could see why this place was always buzzing. Today, it annoyed him, though, does nobody ever work in this town? Usually, he would have enjoyed the loud energy, but not now.

Pete wore black trousers and a white shirt with sleeves rolled up. The greying hair suited him and he knew it. Pete had just returned from holiday in the Maldives with his new girlfriend. He kept droning on about the hut out on the ocean, only accessible via a walkway or via the water. Looking out onto the sea from your bedroom window. Pete sounded like a glossy travel agent brochure.

'Mate, you are quiet tonight'.

He snapped out of his thoughts and grumbled, 'Linda came over this morning and collected some things. She looked different, so full of life.' That had surprised him, he hadn't expected her to look this well. She had always looked after herself, but today her skin seemed brighter and her dark hair shinier.

'Don't worry about it. You won't have any problems finding someone else, Mate. I'll introduce you to some of Mel's friends. You will love them. You can have fun again! Do you remember the party after the Garrison deal? ' Laughing, Pete reminisced.

He remembered that party well. It was the first time he cheated on Linda. They had just sold one of the first developments at the Shoebury Garrison. The military had sold it to them in 2001, and now they were selling off some of the buildings they had developed. They had made a fortune on the sales, but this was the first, and they threw a huge party. Everyone was there.

Linda had left early; their son was ill, and she wanted to get home. Later, Pete, he and some others had met the girls at the Casino down the seafront, and one thing led to another. 'I can remember that night well. Linda almost divorced me back then.'

Pete laughed 'and then she forgave you'.

Yes, she did. It was a difficult conversation, though. One they'd had a few times since, he had to admit.

They opened their first restaurant together on the Broadway in Leigh. Then Linda gave birth to their three children and focused on bringing them up whilst he expanded their business.

He had kept the restaurants, but in 2000, he met Pete, and they moved into property together. Pete was well-connected and full of ideas. Pete was also the one who introduced him to Mike.

They had gotten on straight away. Mike had always been very confident, and how he talked and dressed impressed him. He had swagger. So when he suggested investing in property at the Costa del Sol, it was a no-brainer. He had bought some villas on the Spanish coast. They were in one of those estates especially built for English buyers with white washed walls, terracotta roofs and a pool in the back yard. The manicured front gardens, with tidy walkways and the odd palm tree would attract retirees looking to settle down in the sun, he had hoped.

A year later, it turned out they had been built illegally and needed to be demolished. At that stage, he discovered that Mike hadn't invested at all and had only cashed in on the commission. He had lost a good amount of money. More embarrassing, though, was that he had told his friends about the deal, and some of them had invested, too. Some never trusted him again after that. He had lost a lot of credibility. Mike had disappeared after that, nobody knew what had happened to him.

When he heard the rumours this spring, he didn't believe it at first. Mike had come back to Leigh. He wasn't sure how Linda met him. They knew each other, of course, from back in the day, but not that well, maybe a couple of dinners where

Mike and he talked business and the women caught up on other news.

Linda had now succumbed to the same charm as he did back then. Mike was the reason why she now collected her things from their family home. After all this time, she had decided to leave.

'I can't believe Mike came back. He must have pissed off quite a few people. Have you heard anything?'

'Don't worry about him. I don't think he will stay long.'

'But Linda might go with him. He can't take her. Who does he think he is?'

'There are other fish in the pond. Don't worry. I told you I'll introduce you to some of Mel's friends. They are great fun.'

Through gritted teeth he hissed 'I don't want any of Mel's friends. I won't let Linda go. Don't you get it? Especially not with that loser Mike.' Her leaving him felt like a rejection he couldn't accept. He had never contemplated leaving her and he had always expected her to stay, no matter what. Linda needed a strong man by her side and that was him, nobody else. He was going to decide when this relationship was over, not her.

'Did you know Mike lives down in Marbella now? Huge villa with infinity pool and view of the sea.'

He seethed with rage. Mike had sold illegal houses to him and half of his mates but got himself a luxury villa. His fists clenched.

He was still fuming when they left the restaurant. Staring at his car he sucked in air noisily. There was a long scratch on the side of his new car. He could have punched someone. 'I bet that was this loser! He knows my car. If I see him, he will find out who he's messing with!' His hands shook when he started the car. The engine of the car roared. He loved feeling the strength and power of it.

The woman still lay on the road in the glare of his headlights. Some toiletries had fallen out of her red handbag. He stared at the image in front of him. Squeezing his eyes shut he rested his forehead on the steering wheel, trying to decide what to do next. He had way too many drinks to call for help, but what if the woman needed help.?

A car on London Road sounded its horn and brought him back to the moment.

He felt a wave of rage welling up again, closed his eyes and revved the engine.

SLEEPING BEAUTY STIRS

ADRIAN LACEY

As a child in the '70s, Phil Farthing had been entranced by Sleeping Beauty in the Crooked House at Peter Pan's Playground. That was the name in those days of the funfair by Southend Pier. He was fascinated by the rise and fall of the princess's chest as she breathed in her sleep. He still vividly remembered the purple laced-up bodice section of her dress and its white puff sleeves, plus the rich cedar green of her pleated skirt. So when he returned years later to the same site and Sleeping Beauty tapped him on the shoulder, it's fair to say he was a little shocked. Very shocked, in fact.

But let's back up a bit.

Phil brought his daughter Jessica to Adventure Island, as it was now known, the 'Peter Pan' brand presumably having aged prematurely. Phil had been amazed to see the Crooked House was still around, and he wanted Jess to see Sleeping Beauty – undulating lungs, bodice dress and all – so she could be as intrigued by the princess as he had been around her age. Jess was 11, going on 21. She had the most beautiful long and vibrant beige curls – a shared gift from her mum, who's black, and her dad, who's white. She'd put on her favourite cream mohair sweater with canary yellow swirls and silver gems, and her leggings had a design like someone had hurled green and grey paint at them. Dad, in a red plaid shirt and jeans, had excitedly held Jess by the hand to lead her into the Crooked House – *she* might have said he dragged her in. He was about to point and say, 'And, look, that's where Sleeping Beauty's been waiting for her prince for years!' But all they could see in the bed where the princess used to be were crumpled white sheets, and blankets thrown back as if she'd just popped out to shower.

Jess couldn't pretend she was upset by this absence. Truth was, part of her dreaded her dad's nostalgia trips. She'd looked forward to going on the rollercoasters and stuff. But she quickly tired of her father's observations such as, 'Back in the '70s we didn't have half the things you do today.' Even if it was true, it very often had negative knock-ons, like her dad telling her she couldn't have the latest fashion accessory from SuperDry. 'I mean, it's insane,' she'd tell her friends. 'You know, I actually might phone Childline. Like, for real.'

'Sod this,' said her dad, on being faced by a complete lack of Sleeping Beauty. 'I'll insist on a refund. You can't let these people get away with it.'

'Which people?' said an American-sounding voice behind him. And then the tap on the shoulder. Phil turned to see a young woman with blonde hair (which appeared to be wet), wearing a purple, white and green dress. 'If you wanna complain to my people, be my guest. The conditions here are lousy. I get paid much less than the prince.' Phil was surprised at her American accent. 'And don't get me started on my employers' views on sleep in work hours.'

'Hey – are you *actually* Sleeping Beauty?' piped up Jessica. She was on the other side of the woman from her dad.

The woman spun round. 'Sure – though my real name's Zellandine. Call me Zella.' If it's possible to curtsy ironically, she did. 'You know, I'm a bit groggy. I just woke up. And I think I'm starting my period.' She rubbed her hair with a candy pink bath towel. 'Can we get a coffee?'

So in the garden of the Three Shells Tea Room overlooking a calm River Thames, they got to know each other better.

After she'd found out her new companions' names, Zella asked, 'Is Harold Wilson still Prime Minister?'

'Who's Harold Wilson?' asked Jess. 'Was he the one who got it in the eye at the Battle of Hastings?'

'No that was *King* Harold,' explained her father. 'Harold Wilson was Britain's boss in the 1960s and '70s.' Then to Zella he said, 'Wilson stood down in '76. So you've been asleep for... let me see...' Phil was counting, but seemed to be running out of fingers, '... at least 47 years?'

'No way,' said Zella. 'Jeez. I hate when that happens. I'm real bad at setting alarms. I was hoping for a man to kiss me to wake me up.'

Getting kissed by a guy didn't work out well for a female Spanish footballer a while ago, Phil thought. And Jess wondered how a princess could agree to be kissed while she was asleep. But neither of them said anything.

Phil pushed a plate of doughnuts towards Zella. She put her palm up to indicate she wasn't tempted. 'I gotta get into this dress. People have expectations.'

'But you must be starving,' chimed in Jess. 'You haven't eaten for decades!'

'Uh-uh, but I've been in hibernation. I use less fuel – like a tortoise or a squirrel.'

Jess pictured the princess with the teeth of a squirrel. Then she imagined the princess's pretty head retreating into a shell. Jess tried hard not to giggle.

'Anyways,' continued Zella, 'I'll eat something healthy soon. I don't feel hungry when I first wake up.' She covered her mouth as she yawned, then took a gulp of black coffee. From a concealed pocket in her pleats she produced a packet of cigarettes and an orange plastic lighter. She was putting a cigarette in her mouth when Phil motioned to her to stop.

'No, no, no – you can't do that any more,' he said waving an index finger forbiddingly. 'It's illegal.'

'Illegal? Get outta here!' exclaimed the princess, looking incredulous.

'It's to stop passive smoking,' Jess explained.

'*Passive* smoking? What in the hell's that? I want to *actively* smoke.' Zella looked very sullen.

'You're allowed e-cigarettes outside, away from the restaurants,' Jess went on.

'*E*-cigarettes? I want *A* cigarette. Not much to ask when you've been denied for decades.' Zella looked to father and daughter in turn and saw they were serious. So she put her cigarettes and lighter away with a sigh and a scowl.

There was an awkward pause in which Phil sipped his cappuccino, while Jess noisily hoovered up her bubble tea through a straw. In the distance on this clear day, a huge bright red container ship glided by on its way up the estuary. Phil ran a hand through his thinning black and grey hair. He adjusted his gold round-framed glasses.

'Do you mind if I ask why you have an American accent?' Phil said. 'I thought you'd be from Essex – or, at least, some part of England.'

'Let's just say it's the Disney effect. I was born in Leigh-on-Sea, but I wanna go to Hollywood. There's more work for Brits there if they assume this accent these days. Or so I been told. I've been polishing it so long, I got stuck sounding like this.'

Phil winked subtly at Jess so Zella couldn't see.

'It's also why I have blonde hair,' the princess went on. 'I'm a natural brunette, but Walt changed all that – damn him.'

Suddenly Zella's brown eyes lit up as if she'd thought of something else, and she slammed her white coffee cup down onto its matching saucer with a loud clink. 'Hey – the world must have changed *sooo* much since I was last awake?'

'Oh, it has – lots,' Phil said.

'It's changed loads for me even in the last few years,' Jess added.

'That's good,' ventured the princess. 'Because before there was a whole bunch of strikes, inflation roared away, and people were having real trouble making ends meet. It was quite an unhappy kingdom.'

'Ah –' began Phil. He looked down at his feet. Jess felt her dad's self-consciousness, coughed and looked at her own feet. Then she looked at the princess's feet; Zella was wearing slipper-style shoes of a simple design made from a light brown hide. They were cut in a jagged V-shape where they met the top of her feet which, along with her legs, were encased in white silk stockings.

'I'm afraid inflation and strikes have come back again,' Phil explained. 'And there's a cost of living crisis. You may have missed the best years.' He looked sad.

'But you must have gotten rid of the three-day week, right?' asked Zella.

'These days, a lot of people are go into work on Tuesdays, Wednesdays and Thursdays,' said Jess. 'Dad says they've got a special name.'

'Part-timers?' offered Zella.

'Close enough,' said Phil. He inhaled through his clenched teeth. Then for Jess he explained the three-day working week back in the '70s was to do with the coal miners' strike, which then led to electricity rationing.

'But not everything's getting tougher these days, thank goodness,' said Jess. 'Some things are better for women now. Years ago they didn't even have the vote.'

'That was a bit before the '70s, lovey,' Phil pointed out gently.

'I know, Dad. It was when everything was in black and white, and people moved jerkily. But thanks to Emmeline Pankhurst and the suffragettes, I'm going to study STEMs.' Jess looked really pleased.

'Study stems? You wanna be a gardener?' asked Zella.

'No, no – it means Science, Technology, Engineering and Maths. Nowadays, women can be whatever they want.' Jess had other things she wanted to ask the princess. 'You're the first Zella I've met – where does the name come from?'

'Originally I was in a romantic story called Perceforest,' Zella answered. 'That was a while ago now – the year 1340.'

'Wow,' said Jess.

'Then the Black Death came along and although I avoided it, I couldn't cope with the suffering. That's when I hit the opium.' Zella winced at the memory. 'And fell asleep the first time.'

'You said you were "in a story",' Phil began. 'Does that mean you're an actress?'

'Sure. You got a problem with that?' Zella sounded defensive.

'Er... only that you told Jess you're *actually* Sleeping Beauty.' Phil was trying to piece the evidence together like a TV detective. He wondered how Zella could be both an actress and a princess at the same time.

Jess had moved on. 'So what made you wake up this time, Zella?'

'My meds were wearing off. Britain's industrial relations in the '70s had been getting to me.' The princess looked mournful with the recollection. 'I took drugs to numb the pain – in place of strife.' She then gave out a hollow laugh. 'I popped the "wonder drugs" of the '70s: Librium and Valium. With a side order of Temazepam, Neulactil and Equanil. Oh, and a bit of chlorpromazine. That's Largactil, to you.'

'Blimey,' said Phil. 'It's a wonder you woke up at all.'

'Temazepam sounds like marzipan,' Jess enthused, in-between slurps of bubble tea. 'I *love* it!'

'Trust me, honey, you don't wanna confuse the two. Just say no.' The princess sounded downbeat. 'I got such a sore head now.' She took her cigarettes out of her pocket again, looked guiltily at Phil and Jess, and put them away.

'Seems like the drugs don't work for you,' said Phil. 'Have you thought about therapy?'

'Therapy?!' The princess virtually spat out the word. She

drew back from the table, looking appalled. 'Darling, I might sound American but I'm not a freaking beatnik. Besides, reaching for painkillers is too ingrained now. You may remember in another version of Sleeping Beauty I fell asleep because my finger got pricked by a spindle.'

'Gosh! I remember that story from school,' said Jess.

'An industrial accident?' asked Phil.

'Pre-industrial, honey.' The princess's eyes were fierce. 'It was 1697. And I hit the laudanum hard.'

As she sipped the last of her coffee, Zella looked exhausted. 'Can I get a break from all this thinking? I'm at a funfair but I'm not having any fun. Plus, I'm usually too busy working to get outside the Crooked House.'

'Would you like to go on some rides?' Jess sounded enthusiastic.

'Sure!' Zella was suddenly energised. 'Can we go on the bumper cars?'

'Thing of the past, I'm afraid,' said Phil, regretfully.

The princess looked glum for a moment, then cheered up as she had another idea. 'Okay – how about the waltzers?'

'I don't think they have those any more,' said Jess. 'But there's loads of other rides, Zella. There's the Barnstormer, the Green Scream, the Ramba Zamba, the Screature, the Mighty Mini Mega, the...'

'Wait wait wait! I don't have enough coins for all those,' said Zella, trawling through her purse.

'Coins? No need – we'll get you a wristband like we've got and you'll be covered. We'll go contactless.' Jess was getting very excited.

'Contactless?' queried Zella. 'You mean, we won't touch anything?'

'It's a way of paying, you'll see,' Phil pointed out. 'But Zella *you* shouldn't have to pay at all. Or you must qualify for a staff discount?'

'You cannot be serious!' Zella replied. 'You want me to draw attention to myself when I'm playing hooky?'

Phil looked humbled. Fair point, he thought. He excused himself from going on the rides for now, and got wistful watching Jess spin around like a dervish on the latest hi-tech gear. He thought back to japes with mates in simpler times.

For the grand finale, they insisted on Phil joining them on the infamous ride called Rage. Of course, Phil checked the relevant stats on his phone before boarding – Rage was over 1100 feet long, 72 feet high, and had a top speed of over 43mph. But nothing prepared him for the body shock of the loops, twists and inversions of this outrageous rhubarb-and-custard-coloured ride. It looked like it was built from a huge version of the Meccano metalwork kit he'd had as a boy.

Phil's ears felt overloaded with Jess's and Zella's screams next to him as they were flung into bends, turned upside down and dragged up impossible gradients. After an exhilarating 50 seconds, their car eventually came to a halt and the two others with him relaxed and let out relieved laughter. Eventually Phil worked out that the ear-piercing scream which was still going on was, in fact, his own. He silenced it and sat looking slightly embarrassed.

'That was amazing!' said Jess, as they released their seatbelts.

'Phew!' said Zella, catching her breath.

'Bloody hell!' went Phil, clutching the railings unsteadily as he climbed out of his seat.

'I want to do all those rides again,' said Jess, 'plus the ones we missed.'

'Do we have to?' asked the princess, wearily. She had her hand on her tummy. Phil saw it was moving in and out deeply and quickly.

'What's the matter, Zella?' he asked, concerned the princess was looking a little pale.

'I don't have the energy to do any more rides. I feel disoriented and down,' she replied with a heavy heart.

Jess looked crestfallen.

'Sorry, sweetie,' Zella said to her. 'Plus it's time for my

medication again. If only I could get my hands on some new wonder drugs.'

Phil involuntarily rolled his eyes.

Jess said to Zella, 'I'm still confused. What exactly *are* you?'

Zella touched her shoulder lightly and said, '*You're* confused? How do you think *I* feel?! With this muzzy head I'm not sure of anything. Except, I'm gonna need to rest. Hopefully not too long. A year or two, is all.'

And with that, she said a big breathless thank you and goodbye to her new friends and walked slowly, but purposefully, back to the Crooked House.

THE MEETINGS

RACHEL DINGLE

First thing you need to know is I'm the fucking hero of this story.

No, don't write that. No one will like you. And people have to like the hero of the story I think.

Meeting One

Colin Golditts enters the room. He's late to the meeting. "Sorry I'm late my laptop got stuck under someone else's car."

He sits down and no-one questions it. He must do stuff like this a lot. Accident prone? Full of bad luck? Maybe just a moron?

He then makes a lot of noise getting the laptop out of his bag, putting it on the table, opening it, pressing the power button slowly at first then repeatedly …to then remember it literally just got squashed by a car. He closes the lid slowly which makes an increasing crunching sound.

Definitely a moron.

Lozza is chairing the meeting. She's flouncing up and down, trying to compensate over the noise of laptop boy. "Do you know BLEEP, Colin?"

[Yes I've bleeped my own name out of this story]

They all wave/nod at me. "She's a BLEEP BLEEP"

[Yes I've also bleeped my job out of this story. Imagine if people found out these characters were based on them]

"She's new to the department of BLEEP. Joining us for the first time"

Lozza tries to regain control of the room. There are ten of us. All representing a different department – I know most of them. A few strangers. A quick scan of the room and it's Andrew that stands out. He has yellow hair. Not blonde, I mean yellow, like neon yellow. Like someone has coloured his head in with a highlighter. He seems friendly but I've heard mixed reviews. Next to him is Dew Beer – a softly spoken lady with a fringe that stretches over her mousy features. Every time she blinks she catches the bottom of the fringe, which makes her blink more; she stretches her forehead up to release the hair from the clutches of her eyelashes. A never-ending cycle. Three guys called something like Bob and Rob and Todd. Or Tim, Tom and Ted. Short white male names. They seem tired of this shit.

Coriander wakes up. Apparently it's usual for her to be asleep.

Lozza shouts "Okay let's get started. We need to work out what to spend the money on."

Our company has been awarded a bonus and it's up to these people, in this room, to decide what to do with it.

The discussion winds around and around, moments of progress pushed back by unnecessary caution. By the end of the hour we've decided to have another meeting and create a form to discuss the best way to have these meetings going forward. I offer to make the form. If I seem keen now I can collect my reward later…right?

"BLEEP is sorting the form, Coriander can assist." Lozza passes us a piece of paper. A piece of paper.

Coriander takes it and her pen skips across the page.

I start to suggest perhaps an online system would be more

beneficial, but I catch the eye of Rob/Bob/Tim/Tom who shakes his head three short times and then taps his watch.

Lozza declares the meeting over. A cacophony of noise; scraping chairs, yawns and stretches, and the sound of bags thwacking backs as they're slung over shoulders.

Coriander hands me the form.

"Here you go, I'll leave the rest to you."

I take it. And look at it. Then up at her. Perplexed.

"Sorry what?"

"You can handle it from here can't you?"

I stare at her and then to the blank piece of paper. Blank except for the date in the corner. Then back to her. I go to speak but she's asleep again. Jesus Christ.

<u>Meeting Two</u>

I bring the completed form and hand it out.

No-one makes any remark. I was expecting some push back – I'd completed it outside hours. I'm the only one working part time ffs. They all take one, glance at it and put it to one side. One arsehole says are we sure we want to have a form – can't we just discuss it?

I sit down, looking around the room at these pricks.

We have six weeks to decide what to spend this money on. But there's only one hour in the week where we're all free to meet. So really we've got 6 hours. Minus the one we had last week. Minus the 15 minutes they've just spent ripping up the form they thought was essential last week.

Colin enters – late again – one side of his glasses is missing. No-one mentions it.

There's a bit of chit chat about a drama I know nothing about. Lozza steers us back on track.

We briefly recount the aims of this group, restating who is involved (going around the circle and re-introducing ourselves – I still didn't catch the boys actual names), the date by which we need to confirm what we're doing with the money and the amount of money there actually is. There's a pause. What was it? Are you sure? No-one can agree.

Andrew is insistent he was told this figure. Lozza is flicking and flapping through a frankly insane amount of papers, files and notebooks – tossing them out of her bag like Mary Poppins looking for made up words.

Someone has woken Coriander. She's the most senior person here. She must know. She says she probably does know the amount but is unsure whether she has permission to tell us.

Colin sits forward, as he does the remains of his glasses drop from his nose and he quickly shoves them back up his face as he says rather timidly that we'd been told before so can't see why we can't be told again.

Kayleigh snaps something about protocol and not making assumptions. She's a wild one.

Dew Beer says it was on an email that she was cc'd in but she doesn't have access to her emails at the moment because her system is broken. It's certainly not the only one.

Coriander pulls at her glasses, which hang on a colourful chain around her neck, she looks down her nose at Colin as she shakes her hair from her face and slots the glasses onto her ears. She's never put her glasses on before. Was this a sly dig at Colin's misshapen spectacles?

Coriander spends an excruciating amount of time searching her phone for the email. Her perfectly manicured digit slowly tapping at the screen - like a blind pigeon pecking for food. I nearly offer to help but remember the amount she contributed to the forgotten form. Twice the phone locks and she holds it up to unlock the screen. She pulls a face of such concentration - I assume to aid the face recognition software - staring into the camera as if she's controlling it with her mind. Maybe she thinks that's how it works.

Lozza is desperately trying to motivate the group to carry on whilst Coriander finds the email. She's fighting a losing battle. Kayleigh refuses in case she faces a disciplinary for being involved with something she's not allowed to be involved with. "Can't do much till we know how much we're dealing with," says Rodd /Todd sitting back in his chairs'. "And can't do that till we know if we're allowed to know how much we're dealing with," says Todd/Rodd. They've got each other's backs. Like one big-backed man machine.

Glancing away from the mess that is this meeting, I look out of the window, gazing at the sea. The windows are basically floor-to-ceiling, so I can see the seafront sprawling out seemingly going on forever – I can feel my annoyance start to settle... a little. In the distance I see Rage, the big yellow and purple roller coaster. Rage. Apt. I watch as a car reaches the tip of the highest point of the ride. Teetering, about to go over the edge. Me and this rollercoaster have a lot in common. As I watch the car race down the tracks it seems to me that this part of the ride looks quite phallic actually, jutting directly up towards the sun, significantly taller than the rest of the buildings around it. I wonder if the owner was compensating for something. I mean it is called Rage. My attention snaps back to the room as Coriander makes a distinct chirping sound. She's found the email.

She reads out the amount (Andrew was correct) followed by the confirmation that we are all allowed to know. The irony of the order that information was shared is not lost on me. Coriander folds her glasses and lets them dangle on the front of her blouse. Colin stares at them. Or at least that's what I think he's staring at.

Lozza blinks at her watch. She suggests we all have a think in our own time about the options. A deep intake of breath through the noses of the lads – they all heave backwards away from the table in unison. They're all very busy. This meeting is already an addition to their current vast responsibilities.

The meeting ends. We all filter out leaving Lozza sat at the table staring into space.

. . .

Meeting Three

Postponed. Someone organised it on a bank holiday.

Meeting Four

After thirty minutes going round in circles like a lawn-mower tied to a stick, I suggest we make a list and then simply vote on our favourite

"We can't do that!!" screams Kayleigh.

Hate to say it but I respect her commitment to bullshit.

"We can't vote. It's not democratic – and we have absolutely no time to do this –" Kayleigh repeats

I stand up and walk slowly towards the white board.

Rob / Bob / Tob heads don't move but their eyes follow my path to the front of the room. Cowards. Andrew calms Kayleigh down, "maybe we try this and if it doesn't work we go back to the old method?"

My hand reaches for a pen. A red one. To show I'm serious.

"THERE'S NO TIME!!" Kayleigh has drawn on some past trauma. Reaching into her soul to bring real emotion to her argument. Respect.

I write the numbers 1 2 3 4 5 on the board. And then turn slowly.

"Let's narrow it down to five things."

Kayleigh's crying.

Ignoring her, whilst still appreciating the performance, I look at Lozza. She's at the other end of the table. Looking down at her trademark green fingernails. She slowly raises her head. We lock eyes. I nod. I put my hand up slowly offering her the pen.

She nods. And slams both hands on the table as she stands. Bracelets jangling. The sound of her slamming the table and the door banging open revealing Colin happen simultaneously. A really dramatic moment.

Colin enters carrying a child of about 6 months in a clearly homemade sling. He's sellotaped his glasses to what looks like a spork. Babbling and dribbling, Colin sits down. The broody ones of the group can't stop staring at the baby. The non-broody ones of the group also can't stop staring at the baby – annoyance already spreading across their faces. The commotion that always accompanies Colin's entrance has masked Lozza walking to the front of the room and taking the pen from me.

I sit down and glance at the baby. It's wearing an exact replica of the suit Colin has on.

In the moment my attention is distracted by the small well dressed infant, Lozza has rubbed off the numbers from the white board with one of her long floaty sleeves.

I take the pen in my hand and nearly ram it into one of my eyes.

"I think," Lozza says, taking back control "I think we need to recap. Start again."

I think about ramming the pen into my other eye.

Andrew mentions how little time there is left of this meeting, and questions whether it's a good use of time.

Kayleigh suggests we vote on it. Lozza asks who is up for doing a recap. Five hands shoot up, including herself and Kayleigh. Kayleigh has unsubtly lifted the arm of a sleeping Coriander. "And who is against?"

Mine and four other hands are raised. 5 v 5. Stalemate. We all look at each other searching for a leader, searching for an answer, searching for someone to make it make sense. Then we all slowly turn and look at Colin. And then down at the baby.

"Let's offer the baby two pieces of paper. And written on each one is Recap and No Recap."

Bill/ Bob/ Whatever are suddenly interested. Sports.

"I don't think that is going to work," says Colin. He explains that the baby won't do anything unless given permission. (Maybe it's Kayleigh's baby). We spend the remainder of the meeting coaxing the baby to pick one of the two pieces of paper – to no avail. To be fair to Colin, that baby, whoever it is, is very well behaved.

<u>Meeting Five</u>

Two meetings left. In my exasperation I get into a stand off. I don't understand and no-one can give me an answer.

"There must be a document somewhere that explains the desired outcome from this money."

They look blankly at me.

"There's this pot of money that needs to be spent. There must be. There has to be a list of what it can and what it can't be spent on."

Silence.

"It's a good, valid question BLEEP, but it's never as simple as people think it is."

"I didn't say it was simple. But what's stopping us spending it on a group holiday?"

Kayleigh gasps. And shakes her head in disbelief. Covering her mouth as if she's just heard me say about the time I drowned a kitten for fun.

This idiot not seeing the difference between a point of view and making a point is one thing. But genuinely believing I'd voluntarily spend more time with her? Crazy.

Andrew mentions there had been a fair amount of consultancy on the topic of the funding before it was granted to the company. There's a report somewhere.

I knew my man Andrew would come through.

I ask if we've all read it. Shuffling of papers and re-adjusting of sitting positions.

"Yeh when it came out."

"I've almost certainly, definitely flicked through it."

"It's flagged red on my inbox."

"I think I might have written part of it."

I sigh and suddenly become aware how easily I can

control the rage this incompetency has fired up inside of me. They're doing their best.

"Can anyone summarise it?"

We spend the rest of the meeting making a comprehensive list of what the money can't be spent on. This focused work produces some tangible results.

At the end of the meeting I realise there's been no sign of Colin.

Meeting Six

I know I said I wouldn't. but I worked on the list on my lunch break. I want it to be successful – and every story needs a hero.

"Here's the pros and cons of each of the three suggestions," I declare as I hand out the pieces of paper. As expected only half of them read it.

But I only need half to get on board. Andrew takes the reins. Pushing for a decision. Using some excellent persuasive phrases.

We start to make progress. We've dismissed one of the suggestions. Now it's just between two.

Two proposals. 27 minutes to go.

We go round the circle, skipping sleeping Coriander, and Dew Beer isn't here – and Colin hasn't made his entrance yet. So there's just seven people to listen to.

I say "I prefer proposal one but proposal two has a far more realistic contingency – and with the rise in practical costs associated with this type of thing because of the global situations we're in, it looks like the safer bet. It'd be a shame to give the money to something that can't be completed."

I thought it was succinct. I didn't expect it to start a debate about Brexit and the war in Ukraine.

"I don't think we can entirely blame Putin for pencils getting so expensive."

I get out some crisps. Wait for this to blow over.

"It's also not entirely the Tories fault – there's only so much you can do in ten years."

I crunch five at once.

"What's that got to do with refugees on boats?"

I tilt my head back and tip the crumbs into my mouth.

"I think we need to avoid objectifying Zelensky."

I fold my crisp packet into a triangle the way my dad does. It's calmed down. None of them really understand global politics. Who does? Lozza's asked Andrew his opinion to get the conversation moving again

He says a similar thing to me but avoids mentioning global politics. A true ally.

Kayleigh disagrees with herself.

Tim Tom and Tam can see that agreeing with us means the meeting will be finished on time and they'll be on the winning side. Sports.

I can see the finishing line. The money being allocated to something worthwhile. Hooray.

Coriander stirs.

"That makes sense. And ties into why we disregarded that other proposal."

People nod.

Wait a second. What.

That was mentioned a good twenty-five minutes ago. She's been asleep since the meeting started. How did she hear about the proposal we disregarded? It clicks. She's been faking it this whole time. God damn. I nearly give a standing ovation. It's perfection executed. I make a mental note of this technique. Being present, ticking boxes, but doing absolutely nothing. Fair play to her. A political queen.

Lozza has added the final amendments to the report. We've done it. We've actually done it.

A minute before the end of the meeting, Colin is pushed in on a vertical trolley –his entire body in plaster cast. The two guys wheeling him in stand him up, he rocks briefly and then settles. They give him the thumbs up and exit.

"You missed it but we've agreed where the money is going Colin."

He makes a noise that could be distinguished as a fairly offensive curse word. But at least he's got new glasses.

IN SUPPORT OF

A portion of the proceeds from the sale of this book supports the following charities…

ASPIRATIONS PROGRAM

Aspirations was founded by Marie Edmonds, who has lived experience of addiction, mental health issues, and adverse childhood experiences.

Marie and her team's dedication to professional development and continuous learning is evident in the breadth of their skills and extensive training in addictions, conflict management, complex mental health, and sexual trauma.

Our mission is to empower individuals in their recovery journey from active addiction's harmful effects and assist in ongoing freedom from addiction.

Aspirations is a beacon of hope and support and provides services in four essential programs.

Aspirations Day Program

This is a structured, non-residential, non-religious program led by trauma-informed, trained counsellors and group facilitators. The program runs for at least 12 weeks and can be longer if needed. The program includes process groups, individual therapy and sessions with a key worker.

Carrie's Outreach

Carrie's Outreach is a support service specifically for women who sell sex. For many women, selling sex is a way to fund active addiction, and substances are a way to block out the reality of selling sex. Carrie's Outreach works with other local organisations to provide routes out of selling sex.

Family Support

When someone has an addiction, their family and friends suffer, too. The Family Support service is a group for those who wish to learn more about addiction so they can support someone close to them.

Harley's Space

It was established in memory of a young man, Harley, who tragically lost his life to addiction. The need for a dedicated young person's space became apparent from young adults seeking recovery attending the day program.

Enquiries and Donations - https://www.aspirationsprogram.co.uk/

THE ESSEX WILDLIFE TRUST

There is now an urgent need to tackle the climate emergency, restore damaged habitats, connect our protected areas to the rest of the landscape, and lobby for legislation that places natural heritage at the forefront of policies and forward planning.

We all have a role to play in protecting what's important to us. In order to stop the deterioration of our natural world in its tracks, we need to think globally while acting locally.

We need to create a Wilder Essex. One where wildlife is thriving, every person has access to nature and our habitats are all connected.

Essex should be a safe haven for wildlife and an example to which other counties can aspire. Essex Wildlife Trust has brought back species on the brink of extinction before, and transformed damaged and degraded habitats into havens for wildlife. Creating a Wilder Essex isn't just a vision, we know it's possible.

The Trust is backed by a dedicated team of volunteers and members, and for over 60 years has been tackling environmental challenges covering land, rivers and sea. From ancient woodlands offering a green lung in Southend-on-Sea, to the last place in the county where all three species of heather grow together. Areas of significant natural heritage are protected for perpetuity.

But previously discarded areas have also been brought back to life. The song of the nightingale rings out at the old gravel works at Fingringhoe, while the former landfill site at Thameside is now littered with rare invertebrates and reptiles.

A Nature Recovery Network is not only about connecting our habitats for wildlife, but connecting people with wildlife and green spaces once again. Essex should have boundless opportunities for children to learn outdoors in a natural environment, a place to be independent and confident, a place to be playful and curious, a place to inspire a lifelong love of nature.

It's never too late to learn about its wonders or re-discover your love of the great outdoors. We need to see people of all ages and backgrounds engage with the natural world at every stage of their life.

ACKNOWLEDGMENTS

Huge thanks to Jen Feroze for all her literary wisdom in guiding this anthology to fruition. Massive thank also to Sam Lierens (aka Lizzie Page), one of the founding tutors of Write Club, who has offered so many fantastic insights and given endless encouragement to all the students.

A big thank you to Christine Wyatt, Alison Cottridge, Simon Fowler and the whole team at Create 98 – we would have been homeless without you! Man-of-many-talents Simon also created the fab cover for this anthology.

Above all, thank you to all the brilliant guest tutors who have run sessions for us over the years. Too many to mention, from Authors to Agents, Publishers to Poets, and Playwrights to Prophets, you have been a huge inspiration to Write Club.

Printed in Great Britain
by Amazon

32265985R10086